BROKEN THINGS

PADRIKA TARRANT was born in 1974 and lives in Norwich. She studied sculpture at Norwich School of Art, where she developed an unhealthy fixation with scissors and the work of Jan Svankmajer. *Broken Things* is her first full-length work, reflecting both an interest in surrealism and her own experience of psychosis. She shares her home with a daughter, an ill-mannered cockatiel and far too many animal skulls.

PADRIKA TARRANT
BROKEN THINGS

SALT

CAMBRIDGE

PUBLISHED BY SALT PUBLISHING
14a High Street, Fulbourn, Cambridge CB21 5DH United Kingdom

© Padrika Tarrant, 2007, 2008

First published 2007

Printed and bound in the United Kingdom by Biddles Ltd, King's Lynn, Norfolk

Typeset in Swift 11 / 14

ISBN 978 1 84471 343 1 hardback
ISBN 978 1 84471 409 4 paperback

Salt Publishing Ltd gratefully acknowledges
the financial assistance of Arts Council England

1 3 5 7 9 8 6 4 2

For my friend Charlotte Francis, because I miss her.
For all the precious broken things.

CONTENTS

PADRIKA TARRANT

BROKEN THINGS

DARLING

U NTIL TODAY, I always pushed a pram, just in case I find a baby. People lose them all the time, don't they, so the chances are some day I'll get lucky and pick one up. I'm kind, and ever so patient; a baby wouldn't be badly off with me, I don't think.

I save stuff, keep safe what nobody else cares for, whatever Jesus sends my way. My heart is full of darkness, otherwise I would be an angel, but still he does let me have things, little things like chewed gum and broken bottles, and words. I wrap them in tissue paper to keep them safe, except the words, which are fragile and have to be learned by heart.

So, it wasn't a big shock when I found the dog; I was overjoyed, and sent little thankyous to heaven by the thousand, because a dog is very nearly a baby. He was black and white, and wet with blood, and when I found him he was so vulnerable and wounded that I simply cried. I called him Darling, because that is a good name for someone you love.

When I lifted my Darling from the roadside, the utter looseness of his body shocked me so much that I all but dropped him. His head lolled at a sick angle; he seemed boneless, just a floppy mass of joints. No wonder he needed me so badly. I lowered him into my pram, and as if at some secret sign from God, it began to rain.

1

I wheeled him right indoors; my bedsit's on the ground floor, which is lucky. The landlady is godless and dyes her hair; she hates me because I pain her conscience. I save things from being ruined, and I keep them in my room; she's envious of my vocation.

When I lit the gas fire and turned on the light, I looked down at my Darling. He was wrong, all flat across the ribs where the car's wheel had squashed him, and sort of funny, as if his arms and legs had been attached backwards.

I hunted around the room for plastic bags, and with them I propped him into a better shape, around the sides and under his chin, until his muzzle was resting on his front paws. He had big ears shaped like triangles and a little short tail.

I stroked his poor chest and tried to make it better with my fingers, but in the end I had to pad it out with a Sainsbury's bag, which I fed inside through a slit I made in his skin. I was terrified I'd hurt him, but Darling was so brave, he didn't complain once, just lay quite still and let me help him.

It was after three when I finished, and I was worried, because it's binmen day on a Friday, and I usually go from house to house, making sure only bad things are left for the dust truck. Generally, I start my rounds at five, but in the end, I was simply too tired. My soul was swimming with love, and that just couldn't be a sin.

I slept until nine, but my dreams were odd. I heard Darling in my sleep; he was dreaming too, of headlamps and screechy brakes, and he whimpered for hours. I was trying to find him in my room, but somehow I couldn't; all that I could get my hands on were clumps and clumps of dog hair.

When I said Good morning to my Darling the next day, I was shocked at the state of him. His fur was clotty with blood, and it wouldn't clean up, not with shampoo, not even with bleach. Eventually, an idea struck me, and I tore up newspaper and made him a brand new skin, layered with glue. He was stiff inside his fur already, and so he didn't mind at all, having a paper shell. The dents on his surface smoothed out beneath it, and I made him sculpted flanks and the muscular haunches of a prophet dog. He needed a more dignified tail, so I carried on where his left off, and made it curl like a whip along his side.

Darling took ages to dry, even with both halves of the fire on full, and during the night he whined. I began to worry about the landlady, but the noise didn't seem to bother anyone. By the next day his carapace was almost hard, but poor Darling had begun to seep and stain it, and at any rate he didn't like being all covered with bad news writing from the paper, so I looked among my piles and boxes for paint. I gave him a lovely black enamelled coat, and I varnished his eyes, which I had left uncovered so he would be able to see.

All that night I worried about Darling's eyes. What kind of mother would I be, I thought, if I did the wrong thing? God would never trust me again. Perhaps he would be better off with new ones, now he was becoming so beautiful? In my dreams I tried to catch him, but his flesh was soft and loose as wet cotton wool and my fingers went right through.

In the end, I got up before my window grew light. Darling's eyes were going brown and caving in. I rushed about in a panic, piling up milk bottle tops and buttons and five pence pieces, but none were right. Then a thought came to me from somewhere perfect, and I snapped the thread of

3

my necklace. Darling gazed at me with his golden amber eyeballs, and I was so happy I could have flown to heaven.

That day was like Christmas lights; I found a bit of gold leaf to gild his eartips and I dabbed in a blue scrolled nose with a tiny paintbrush. I stuck tinfoil in strips to give my Darling claws for his feet, and made a clever, latticework design over his spine with picture wire. I left the fire on high to help him dry, and went to bed exhausted.

But to my horror, Darling howled all night and the air in my bedsit grew fat with stink. In my sleep I gagged on it; I coughed and retched myself awake a dozen times. When I woke in the morning, I jammed cushions along the gap beneath the door to stop the smell of Darling crawling down the hallway, and I poured a bottle of violet scent over him.

I wracked my brains for things to make my Darling nice; I glued little paper stars along his front paws and sang him songs to cheer him up. I let him wear my charm bracelet around his proud dog neck, and I decorated the pram like a bier with toilet paper roses. I cut out happy faces from magazines and stuck them over the places where my Darling's body was oozing.

He was so unhappy; he barked and yelped that night, fit to break your heart. I still tried to catch hold of him as I slept, but all my hands could close upon were bones. He yammered louder than the radio on full volume, and so loud I didn't hear the landlady come to the door. The neighbours had phoned the police; I got a note, but it went underneath the cushions so I didn't see.

In the darkness, my Darling spoke. With a voice like wet leaves; he told me that he hated me. I couldn't believe it, I just couldn't, but then a godly wisdom came upon me and

4

I knew what I had to do. I forced myself to be happy, for my Darling's sake, and before five I left the house, with him staring out from the pram like a prince dog.

I stopped along the roadside, wherever there was something beautiful, and I filled the space at Darling's feet with flowers from gardens and crisp packets and handfuls of fresh green grass, until he looked like a holy effigy from Walsingham, processing down the street on a feast day.

We watched the sun come up, Darling and I, as we stood on the kerb at the spot where I had found him first. Although I'd loved him, my Darling had not loved me back, and I knew that it was only kind to return him to the place where I had found him. Even so, I could not quite find it in my heart to strip him of all his glory, for surely love is a perfect thing, even if futile?

We waited there for an hour, in a morning that was horrible with bird song, until a car came past, and then I pushed my Darling out in front of it.

ANATOMY

INSIDE ME IS a secret; I am keeping it calm, soothing its splinters and bones among my intestines and a warm soup of blood. When I walk, it balances perfectly.

My secret likes the campus, and I take it here often, even though the people that I used to know have all gone now. All except for Finn. I drink hot chocolate in the refectory, and when it's warm, I sit on my coat on the lawns. I bring my textbook everywhere I go, and when the afternoons are sunny, the pages are bright enough to blind. The students sit in gangs of five, or else they come alone and try to read. Some have secrets of their own: you can tell by the way they hold their heads.

I keep my secret underneath my skin. It nestles there behind my liver, piercing a membrane, and to pass the time, it ticks in time with the tocking of my heart.

Inside the gentle squish of fat, my secret is growing, my alien child. A stethoscope might find it, diagnose its jaggy pulse, but there is no one to diagnose but me.

I spend a lot of time at the Pathology Museum. It's always quiet, except when they do lessons in here; they don't let the public in off the streets, you understand, it's not a freak show. They think I'm a medical student: I was, in point of fact, but not for very long. Still, I showed the man at the desk my student card the first few times, and after some weeks he stopped asking to see it. I nod to him every day, and smile; he always says, Good morning.

I come to stand among the jars, and breathe the clean air among the cases and wax models. I spend a lot of time drawing, too. Often, I will lean my back against an empty wall, and crook my arm until it makes a sort of shelf for my sketchpad. It would be more comfortable to sit on the floor. But I wouldn't want to disturb my secret, because if I move too quickly then it digs me, jabs with its corners. It doesn't want me to forget it; my secret wants to hurt.

My tutor was a prophet, you know, with silver hair. He said we were to call him Finn: no standing on ceremony. At the first dissection class I was worried that I might disgrace myself somehow, vomit perhaps; the thought had scared me. But, when Finn's long hands laid out the digestive tract, I was euphoric, having glimpsed the universe.

The open body is a rare flower, with thick peeled petals, and yet more petals within. I heard once that the mother of a god looked down his throat and found that all the universe was there: stars and shopping malls and death and horses, all quivering and vulnerable, trembling like an epiglottis.

At half term he asked to see me. There was something in his look, something peculiar; at the time I misread it. I was anxious, of course, convinced that I had done something wrong. I barely slept that night; I passed the time in bed with my textbook, revising, as if I might get through 'til morning, if only I could learn enough. I dreamed of Finn, for just a moment. His teeth were very white. I woke, startled, with my cheek against a diagram, when one of my housemates flushed the toilet.

When I stand before the mirror naked, I can see the

beauty tracing though me: the deep and shallow colours, and the calm, soft masses. My secret sets off my organs like an expensive brooch, asymmetrical and daring.

When Finn came past today, he didn't see me. I saw him though: he was glistening red and grey and blue; the bones in his face were the soft yellow of piano keys. I saw the jump of his oesophagus as he swallowed, and then I ducked behind a lime tree.

The affair was brief, if you could call it that. He adjusted his tie, clawed his fingers through his hair. He seemed to have forgotten that I was there. I gathered up my coat and stuff, and left. He didn't look up, just picked up a biro and began to drum the table with it.

I didn't go home right away. My housemates would all be there, arguing and eating toast and watching children's TV. I found myself at the Museum instead, hunting among the jars and plastic anatomical models, frantically looking for something. It got dark and the cleaner came in and cleared her throat, but I still hadn't found it, so I went to the house and crept up to my room.

Later, in the bath, I spread out my hand, covered in bubbles, and then I dunked it, splash, and pulled it out again. As the water streamed away, I recited my fingers like a poem: the bones, tendons and major nerves. At the wrist was the tender bloom of a bruise.

That first night, the secret formed; it sang like a gale through a cracked window. By the weekend I was afraid that I was pregnant. I took tests, dozens of them, until the people in Boots and Superdrug started giving me weird looks. I wasn't, of course; no baby is made of blades and edges and bits of tooth enamel.

I didn't attend any tutorials after that. As the months wore on, I found that I didn't have time for lectures anyway; I'd hit on something new, undiscovered: the physiology of a secret. When they sent the letter to say I'd failed the year, I didn't care.

I sent drawing after drawing to Finn, always to scale, showing the cartilage and claws and locks of matted hair. I didn't need a scalpel; my secret was so painful that I could feel its contours underneath my skin, just as if I had swallowed needles. After the third one, the envelopes started to come back unopened. I sent them anyway.

Sometimes I would creep into the Lecture Theatre and sit at the back. Sometimes, Finn would catch my eye, and then flick quickly back to the whiteboard. For a long time, I wondered why he didn't just have me thrown out; then it dawned on me that he was afraid of me, of the secret.

These days I'm much more discreet. I wouldn't like to be banned from the university; there isn't really anywhere else to go. So, I'm polite, friendly to the refectory staff; I give them cards at Christmas. They think I'm rather sweet.

There is death in the museum, and order too, that gives it balance. Every pain is catalogued, lined up, made pure and clean in glass cases and bell jars, until it's hardly a pain at all. There is every syndrome here except my own; I have looked: carefully; scientifically; systematically. There aren't any secrets in the Path Museum. Even so, it's nice inside, and out of the rain on wet days. I am at home here. My secret belongs here too.

COFFINWOOD

THEY ARE NOT the dead, although they look it. They look like the dead because they dress like them; they wear their three-piece suits, and favourite outfits, and First Communion dresses. It's all they have to wear; if it weren't for the borrowings from the people in the cemetery, the poor things would go naked. Corpses don't really need warm clothes.

It is so cold underground. They only have little shacks to keep themselves warm; they make poor little houses, out of coffinwood and tree roots, and they shiver and sigh and their children cry in winter.

They don't dare have fires, you see, a fire might suffocate them with smoke, or bake the soil so hard that they'd be entombed in their tunnels and holes. And they're shy; they don't want to be discovered by the light-dwellers; they'd hate to pose a nuisance. So they make do, by and large; the reckless ones creep out sometimes though, to stand underneath the streetlamps and dry their mouldy clothes.

When I was all but a kid myself, I met a coffinwood child, in a green-patched bridesmaid dress, with mushrooms in her hair instead of flowers. I was a lonely teenager back then; when I saw her I was not afraid.

I'd been squatting on the grass behind the stairwell, listening to the rush hour beyond the boundary wall. There were no stars. You don't get stars if you live in the city.

You do see foxes though, sometimes, especially on the estates where there's a bit of grass and foliage that the council men maintain. I was in my first real home, with my Housing Benefit and my Income Support all in place, and although the flat was titchy, the freedom made me feel like a child playing hide-and-seek in an empty house. After the noise and radios and cigarette-coughing of the hostel, I would have died for a pet, but they weren't allowed.

So, I thought I'd recruit myself a hedgehog, or a fox, or at least someone else's cat for half an hour a night, and I began to leave bread and milk in the shadow behind the stairwell.

After a week, I found that I had come down to an empty saucer, and I was elated to have made contact with some other living thing, something with warm skin and a soul. I waited all day, patient and nervous, and when the sun went down at last, I sat in the dark beside my dish, breath bated, desperate for a friend.

The green by the flats is raggish and hummocky as if it's full of moles. The stairwell light had a timer on it, so once I had adjusted my coat and lit a fag and settled myself, it went off with a silent pop. All I could see for ages was the coloured tip of my Marlborough.

Well, ten minutes more, and the bum on my jeans had soaked right through, but there was enough light borrowed from the streetlamps to see quite clearly, but colourlessly, as if everything is remade at night in bluegrey.

There was a tiny tearing sound, like snapping grass roots, and a slim hand appeared in the lawn, quite suddenly, creasing turf outwards like a door made in several pieces. I sat, unbreathing, with the glowing end of my fag cupped in my palm, and watched a child unfold herself from the ground like a question.

Then, she crept towards the dish of milk between us, and held it to her face like a cup, before she caught my eye and fled, quick as anything. When her little ankle vanished through the hole in the ground, and the grass was nearly flat, I put out my fag and gathered up the broken fragments of saucer, shaky and smiling.

That day was knotted up with my probation officer, and trying to sort out a Social grant for a fridge, because you're not entitled to money for one, not automatically, unless you're a diabetic, which I'm not. I had a headache all afternoon; the daylight scrubbed my eyes raw. I could barely stand the wait 'til dusk.

I left more milk out, and chocolate Hobnobs instead of bread. On the way to Tesco's I stopped at the Oxfam shop too, and bought some little woolly tights and a jumper, and I left those on the grass as well. The following morning they were all gone, but there was a gift for me in their place: toadstools, arranged like a bouquet and tied up with slimy yellow ribbon.

The second time that I saw the coffinwood child, she didn't run at the sight of me. She was thin and white as a sparrow's bone, but with those stripey tights on and a sweater over her bridesmaid dress, that almost reached her knees, she seemed less fragile, protected by the padding.

She came out of the ground and stood before me, quivering like a taut, plucked string. I got to my feet very gently, and handed her a dish of vegetable soup. She sniffed at it for a few moments, blinking huge mauve eyes at me, until finally she risked a sip. Then she bolted it like a greyhound with a stolen hotdog. When she smiled, her teeth lit up her muddy face like a candle.

She sang to me that night, sang in the wetblack language of soil. Although the words were senseless to me, I found myself seeing her story, or rather feeling it with the skin of my fingertips, because the songs were dark and buried and sunless.

She sang about her coffinwood house, all made of splintered pine and mahogany and metal handlepieces, with a brass plate on the front door that read In Loving Memory. But the wood from coffins is narrow and sparse, and the silk from coffin linings is hardly enough to wrap a baby in. I learned what it is to be cold to the bone, and also the strange blind beauty of things beneath the ground.

I spent the night behind the stairwell with the coffinwood child, trying to teach her English whilst she braided my hair into dozens of tiny plaits, sealing each at its tip with wet clay. Eventually I fell into a goosefleshed, shuddering sleep.

After dawn, I woke up with a jolt; an ambulance man was lifting up my eyelid and shouting in my face. Someone had seen me sleeping, and thought I was a junkie, overdosed or dead already. They made me go indoors, and didn't leave until my social worker arrived.

She stayed ages. In the end, I ate beans on toast to please her, and promised that I would have a bath. When she'd gone, I went into the bathroom and looked at myself in the mirror, squinting underneath the lightbulb. I was honest and dirty as a burrowing creature; I filled the tiny room with the scent of compost. I didn't want to wash after all, and so I wandered back outside like a sleepwalker.

I didn't realise it, but my social worker hadn't actually left; she was outside, talking on the phone in her car. She must have seen me walking round the back of the stairwell, I suppose.

There was no coffinwood child when I went there to look, when I shouted down into the patchy turf that I wanted to come and live with her. If she'd teach me her life underground, I said, then I would get her dry clothes, dry blankets, stuff with which to build a better house. I'd steal chocolate for her, and milk for her baby brother.

But she ignored me; the green between the flats rang with the noise of her ignoring. Please, I called to the coffinwood child, Come and be my friend and I'll share my life with you! But all the coffinwood child did was to fill the housing estate with silence.

I hadn't any spade for digging, but still I clawed with my fingers where the grass used to fold like a door in several pieces; I dug until my social worker called for the police to come and make me stop.

ASCENSION

WHEN HEAVEN WAS ready for her, Victoria was not afraid. The call had been low and soft as the onset of winter, and whispered by the pigeons on the green outside her flat. There is holiness everywhere, and Victoria had been blessed by heaven to see it a little earlier than the poor, precious people of the world.

Victoria had been preparing herself, all these months, as she plaited her hair in the evenings and listened at the open window for the liquid speech of birds; as her breath turned to vapour and her lap grew wet with dew. She tried not to sleep, for it was only the weakness of flesh that made her sleep; but even so, from time to time she would start awake, catch her head as it toppled forward. Then, she would wash her face at the sink, and repent.

Victoria kept her vigil all through November; she read the first signs of the end-time in the coded blooms of fire in the night, and the week when the man two doors to the right had begun to wear gloves outside. She was not foolish, however; she understood full well that the reds and blues in the sky were fireworks. Even so, it pleased heaven that some things in the world were both themselves and something else at one and the same time, like the gentle family of rats that lived with her to test her charity.

They had come to love each other: the playful tumbling

rat-children and their patient mother with her dark, wet eyes. Rats are by their nature close to angels: the thoughts of God himself are echoed in the tremble of their whiskers. Victoria and the rats had watched the ebbing of the month through the window, and they all prayed together when the nights grew dark. Their prayers would blend at nightfall, and drift out into the sky, or else collect in the air near the ceiling like fragrant smoke.

The second sign had come when the housing officer had knocked on the door and tried to persuade her to close her windows and turn on the heating. Victoria loved the housing officer, of course she did, but then she did have the sanctity of her home to consider. In the end, the housing officer had wet her ankles, standing in the melting frost of the grass as she tried to see past Victoria and into the flat.

She informed Victoria that several tenants in the block were having problems with vermin. She said it very carefully, even put her hand through the window and laid it on Victoria's shoulder, in case the news should shock her. Victoria smiled, gazed into the housing officer's eyes with love until she began to blush and pulled her hand back outside. Victoria's love followed her across the grass to the car park, and the mother rat chanted a benediction as she went.

She heard the third sign on the morning TV, as it fed dully through the wall from next door, in the sing-song droning of voices and adverts. She poured herself one last, flat glass of lemonade and sipped it slowly as she sat at her window. Last summer, as Victoria had felt the coming of the call from heaven, she had endeavoured to become as insubstantial as she could; still, these things could only be accomplished by stages.

Until September, she had lived upon tins of clear soup, but when the rats had come to watch over her she knew that it was time for her to drink only lemonade. Only transparent things are truly pure, and life is all pollution; to achieve true serenity one must become as ice. When she eventually finished her drink, it was night again, and Victoria sat at her window and watched as microscopic angels inscribed patterns of frost on the inside of the pane.

After that, all that passed her lips was water, as for three days more she remained in the shell of her body, in the shell of her little council flat on Wellington Green: three days entombed. The rats grew thoughtful, and perhaps a little sad, for they knew that their time of quiet kinship was at an end; still, they did not grudge Victoria her call.

After the dark, it snowed; Victoria had known it would, for that is the way of heaven. The windowsill and the green outside were thick with whiteness so cold and so flawless that it made her quick with joy. She took her leave of the rats; they bowed their tiny wise faces to the carpet. The very smallest of the children begged a liberty; he tiptoed right up to Victoria and softly bit the hem of her garment. She forbade him not.

The coming of the snow was the final sign. Victoria went into her spare room, and she wound her unclothed body in an arctic swathe of net curtain, and when the sun went down, she trod on bare feet into the perfect square of snowy grass outside her window, and she lay down upon it, waiting for the stars to take her with them.

GOD

OD IS EVERYWHERE. You can find God in the most
unlikely places. That's what the pastor used to say, at
the born-again church; then he said that I had a devil
in my heart, so I quit going after that.

There are far too many churches in Norwich anyway: the
old ones made out of stone with dead angels in the church-
yards, the little ones in houses, and the big community hall
things where they all put their hands up in the air. Build-
ings full of people, all praying at the tops of their souls'
voices. It's bloody deafening.

I wouldn't like to be God, I always thought, with all those
people shouting at him and talking in tongues. It's bad
enough for me, walking down the street with all that praying making racket on the airwaves. There are so many, more
than you'd think, pleading and wheedling for a favour.
Between six and eight in the evening most of them are
children, saying grace at dinner tables and then kneeling by
their beds. Hundreds of little voices whisper all at once,
begging for sleep, reciting words they barely understand.
Gentle Jesus meek and mild. Some of them are terrified.

The worst though, the very worst are the prayers for the
sick. Cancer is the one that makes them cry. Lord, heal him;
Father, pity me; save me, now and at the hour of my death.
My bus stop is right opposite the hospital, the Community

one, and I can't get into town unless I stand there every day, sick and reeling with the begging and the curses from the geriatric beds. I insulate my ears with cotton wool; that deadens it a bit. I daren't leave the flat on Sundays.

A month ago, there was a massive thing at the cathedral; people came in on coaches, and they celebrated the war, or the dead, or something. Those Anglicans chant in unison, don't they, and the noise is so compressed, so dense, that it's louder than when you turn on the stereo and it's accidentally been turned up to full volume, and you jump like you've been shot. Louder than that.

Even out in Bowthorpe, where I live, the shouting and the praying was so awful that I just wanted to bury my head. When the phone went, I picked it up but I don't know who it was or what they wanted, because the receiver resonated with everything else and there was a feedback whistle so high that even when I screamed I couldn't hear my own voice, let alone anyone else's.

Well, I thought I was going to lose it any moment, so I heaved the phone out of the wall to shut it up, and I put on my big thick duffel coat. I got my special headphones (nobody speaks to you if you've got headphones on), and I plugged my ears with new cotton wool and masking tape, then I put them over the top. I trailed the wire into my pocket so it looked as if I was listening to something.

After that I ran. I went away from town as fast as I could, and whenever I had to stop and catch my breath, it was a little bit better. I didn't really have a plan, but I followed the direction where it got easier every time, until I found that I had come to the allotments. I went in the gate and started walking along the path between the oblongs of vegetables and sheds. It's best where there are least people, because the prayers echo in all their skulls and make it worse.

On the edge of one patch there was a bonfire. I bet they aren't allowed to make fires. There are probably rules. Even so, there was one there that afternoon: weeds and newspapers spat and cussed in the flames like a pissed old man. That was where I came across God.

God isn't what you would have expected. He wasn't all powerful, and mighty, and omniscient and all that; He was just a little baby, the oldest baby in all the universe. He had a plastic clip on His umbilical cord and He was all washed over with blood and mucous as though He had had a difficult birth and His mother had bled to death. He was crying. I was a bit taken aback.

Then it all went quiet, suddenly, just like that. The people at the cathedral had all finished their prayers and were shaking each other's hands and nodding to each other as they left. The relief was unimaginable; I felt like a puppet with the strings cut. I sat down on the path; it wasn't too damp. God was still wailing.

I didn't really want to talk to God right then, so I rolled a cigarette instead. When I had smoked it halfway down (I lit it with my lighter in case it was rude to use the bonfire), God stopped crying, quite gradually. He had the hiccups. He rolled over from His back to His side so He was facing me. We looked at each other, God and me.

God was incredibly small, like the premature miracle babies you see on the news sometimes, that fit inside the palm of the doctor's hand. I felt a bit sorry for Him. He kept curling His tiny fingers into fists and then opening them out again. His skin was red, and thin as nylon tights; through it little blue veins pulsed. God's knees were bent right up against His tummy and His feet were crossed at the ankles. His scalp was soft with feathery black down.

Well, by then the evening was getting chilly, so I put my hood up and shifted in as close to the bonfire as I could without getting singed. The night turned black by degrees until the only light was from God and the fire. It occurred to me that the leaves and stuff that were burning should have broken down to ash by now and the fire should have been just a smoulder. Instead, it was as blazing as it was when I came wandering in here. I think that He is meant to have played that trick on someone else before.

A baby in fire light: there's a curious thing. When eleven o'clock had come and gone I risked taking off my earphones. The praying had gone down to a few despairing sighs and was as peaceful as it ever was. The fire roared. God whimpered and chewed His fingers, His eyes, blue as blankets, were fixed intently on me. I sat and smoked, my face dry with the heat. The city started filling up the sky with the glow from zillions of streetlamps.

I had begun to doze where I was, sitting up, when God finally spoke. Pick me up? He said, and raised His arms a little towards me. I rubbed my face and answered What? I wanted to be dead certain that I had heard Him. Please, said God, Pick me up.

Well, I said to God, There's a lot of people who think they need you. I gestured vaguely toward the city and the cathedral. And then, you turn up here, tiny and crying. I'm sorry, whispered God. I'm sorry. It's not my fault. Please pick me up. I'm so frightened.

I sighed hard at that and began to roll another fag. God looked at me with His great pale eyes and His bloodstained face and began to weep, not like a baby but like a person, like anybody. Like me. God is a baby and is oh-so scared.

Just then a single voice from a single prayer crystallised like frost in the air between us. Make it end, said a woman. Please just make it end. God put His fists into His eye sockets and sobbed. I'm sorry, said God. I'm so sorry, and the woman and her Creator each recited their pain. The woman dwindled her prayer into silence. God hid His face for an hour.

I began to pick up twigs and bits of leaf from the ground and feed them into the fire. Eventually, God said, Pick me up? Pick me up, please? And His little voice was as old and exhausted as bones. I felt sadder than anything in all the world; too sad for tears; too sad for breathing, almost. I looked at Him and said, Why should I pick you up?

To care for me, said God from the guts of the fire. Because I am a little baby and because I am sorry. Please pick me up. Please love me. I am a little baby and I am so frightened. Take me home with you and love me. I'll be good. I'll not give you trouble. Pick me up? Pick me up, please? And God cried and pleaded and said He was sorry; and He was, you could tell He really did mean it.

It was just before the dawn came that I reached into the fire to rescue God. He was too slippery to keep hold of, especially when I began to bleed. My coat caught light and I tried to get a grip on God and He just said, I'm sorry, I'm so sorry, and I tried and tried to save Him until I lost consciousness. Just before I did, I could have sworn that I heard Him laughing.

HIGH

For today, if you like, I'll be a girl. I'll have two hands for you, and, let me see, I'll have brown hair, long hair that isn't brushed and flicks into my eyes unless I hold my head to the side. If it makes you happy then I'll be seventeen years old. I will wear ice-washed jeans; I'll carry a windproof lighter, which I stole. I'll even have a name if you want. Why not call me Sarah. I'm not changing my eyes though; I'm keeping those.

Yesterday, and the day before that, I was a magpie, turning on thermals like a black and white kite in air. My mind was small and sharp as a craft knife tip, and red. When I spread my feathers, I could scribble poems in the air, so clever and so sad that the people in the market didn't know that I was there. Before you made me sit and talk to you, before these pills, I was nothing but a pair of wings in the sky.

Before today I was quick as silver, and I knew the secret things that hide among the city's pieces. When I was a bird, I was cunning and magic, and a mystery to the world. Before you gave me a blanket to wear, I was narrow like a dart; I could throw myself at people's heads, and spin away at the very last moment and vanish.

From the top of the town hall clock, the world is flat and hardly there. The sky is a landscape, huge, invisible,

23

made of light and music, with great empty cathedrals and mountain ranges. I knocked my head on an outcrop of nothing, smacked against the gusting morning, and I fell. If you want, we can pretend that I'm a girl, just until my wings are mended.

SCREAM

AFTER YOU'RE DEAD, the world becomes like gelatine, made of thickened edges and little more, the smudged blueprints of trees and houses and cars. When you're dead, the world is translucent at best, and you can see at last to the rotten core of things. Trudie can see right through to the rotten core of things.

When you're dead, all there is to do is wait, as your body grows into tracery, and your skin, and everything you learned, and the shoes you bought in the sales, and your pretty tawny hair, all of this, blossoms into nothing.

And, as Trudie turns to nothing, her mind grows hard, and sharp, and clear as buried glass, and she hoards the nothing of herself because that is all she has to hoard. After thirty-two years of mousey patience, comes twenty-five of rage, with centuries more to rage through.

Beside the bus route, before Saint Ladoc's Hill, where the Exxon garage clings to its rough hip, the summer evening will not give in to dusk, and the air is sodden. There's a rain-bitten footbridge, all rust and reddish paint, where resentful school kids troop above the main road, cold and smeared in hockey mud, ready to clamber back up the hill to school and communal showers.

The playing field is churned all year with tyres and football boots. On Sundays, there's usually a market, where sly-faced men sell each other ripped-off DVDs, and watch from the corners of their eyes.

Trudie is folded against her legs like an ironing board because the hole that Philip dug for her was round rather than long, and he stuffed her in carelessly, inside a scrubby bit of hedge.

There's a dog in the playing field, black as newsprint text, loping in lines; river and rain water in his pelt. He is explaining to his master, tracing the route that Philip dragged his wife, from car boot to shovel hole.

It's not in any earnest way; the dog doesn't care, but that's the sort of thing that dogs like. They love patterns of death; it comes from thousands of years of tracking wounded things across ancient plains. The thought of it makes the dog happy, he licks his chops; then his owner swears at him, so he goes to heel.

Philip lives in Norwich these days. He's seventy next week, and the flesh won't stay on him any more. His glasses are folded on the locker, and his wristwatch too, which is about to stop. The nurse has left him a jug of water, and the ice is dissolving slowly.

His skin is all but transparent now, and the lines of bone and vein are written like tracery on the backs of his hands. Nobody has cut his fingernails; they are yellow and rather long. He is a good patient: gently spoken, grateful for the attention. They think he's a sweet old boy.

Trudie had loved her new shoes. She stole pennies from her husband, sometimes whole ten pences, and she kept them buried in the garden, in a net bag meant for protecting tights in the washing machine.

She didn't have money in the last years, not after Philip

dictated her resignation letter to the laundrette, where he made her call the manager a horrible name and make mocking remarks about her mastectomy. As Philip waxed lyrical, Trudie's poor pen could hardly keep up. He made her fill three whole pages, and then got a fresh pad so she could write to Cecily, her one remaining friend, demanding that she never contact Trudie again.

So, those pennies were precious, collected one by one from the change she took from his pockets when she washed his clothes. It took her eighteen months to save £7.99 for a pair of shoes. They were shiny and black and made to look like crocodile skin, with a big goldy buckle on the front that didn't attach to anything. They were fashionable back then, and Trudie didn't care that they looked weird with her dowdy seventies dress and kitchen-scissors haircut. She knew that Philip wouldn't notice them because to him she was furniture.

When Philip thinks of what happened, he finds that he is blameless. He hadn't meant to actually kill her, it was just a bit of casual cruelty, like kicking a cat. He saw her on the staircase and her face was so stupid, so haggard, so perpetually crestfallen, that he told himself later that any-one might do the same.

One well-aimed foot as she neared the top of the stairs, loaded-up with folded ironing. Well, the moment was virtually comedy. Eric Morecambe would surely have done the same.

The look that she gave him as she tumbled slowly back-wards was priceless. When she didn't move at the bottom, he was annoyed, but at the same time intrigued by the new project presented to him: getting away with it.

Trudie is so uncomfortable, even though the soft parts of her that used to jam against the hole have dissolved, and the dress that rode right up against her back is just a loosish mat of fibres. Her new shoes still pinch her heels, even though her heels are only bone. Her skeleton is holding together with ligaments and hatred. Her anger withers the grass in a circle round her.

Then a car goes by, and its radio flickers out of tune as Trudie's fingers catch the airwaves for a fraction of time. A bus moos past afterward, and slows for the traffic lights. The rooks gutter to one another as the dark rises, and Trudie is so eaten with fury and rot, that she begins to scream; her screaming interferes with the TV transmitter at Kingswood.

All she has left to her name are her nothingness and the buckles from her shoes. The shouting rooks join in with her hollering for half the night.

SKIN

I T CREPT UP on me slowly, the thing with my television. I
think it started at the tail end of winter. The central heating was no good; I spent a freezing month in my bedsit
while the landlord fobbed me off with promises and an oil
radiator that doubled my electric bill in one go. It never did
get sorted out; in the end I left before it was mended, if it
ever was.

At first the screen turned filmy; I put it down to conden-
sation, and wiped it every morning, worried that water
might get into the works. It was an ancient thing, black and
white, with one of those tuning dials you had to turn to
change the channel. I bet it was older than me, that television, with its plastic wooden panelling and little round
aerial. It came with the room, like the one-ring burner on a
gas bottle and the spiders who ran about the walls like leggy
ghosts. I loved the TV, warder-off of street noise and evil
spirits; when I had it up loud I couldn't hear the man below
me bellowing at his wife.

It was so cold. I used to sit all day underneath the duvet,
drinking Bovril with boiling water. Giros were every other
Thursday. I hated walking outdoors, among the people with
their hard faces and the cars that chased in fatal spirals on
the roundabout. You don't know where you are with people:
one minute they're ever so nice, and the next, well, it could

be anything. Some of them think so loud you can hear them, accusing you of all sorts.

The residue on the television built up slowly. One morning I knelt in front of it with my damp cloth and instead of scrubbing at it, I put my hand on the screen. It was almost warm, and it had a texture to it like some sort of membrane, like the tiny film of cells you can peel from between the layers of an onion: thin as thought, queasy to the touch and infinitely vulnerable. There was a tiny network beneath it, little grey trackways like a medical diagram.

I'd had it on all night; I always did, for the company, turned down quiet so the people downstairs wouldn't complain. The breakfast programme was on; a weatherman waved his arms vaguely at Wales, prophesying low pressure. I put my hand up to the television once more, and this time I scraped my nail through the thin smeary covering.

It bled. The long drag of my fingernail split it like skin, leaving a ghastly line of clear screen that welled at the edges and drooled deep red in one clotting trickle. I was horrified. Somewhere there was a first aid kit; this too had come with the room. I heaved out an armful of clutter from underneath the bed and found it among the clothes and bits of useless paper.

I didn't know quite what to do. I knelt in front of it for ages, my belly hollow, while I spread out the contents of the little green packet. Eventually, I dabbed at the blood with cotton wool, terrified that the wound would sting. It looked better when it was cleaned up. After some thought, I applied a sticking plaster, smoothing it gently down. I looked up at the injured TV, wondered if I should say something to it, but didn't.

I watched it all that morning; the pink fabric strip obscured the top right hand corner of the picture and kept me tearful with guilt. Eventually I began to doze in front of Neighbours when the landlord knocked at the door.

He leant on the jamb and swept his eyes over the room as he said something about refurbishing the heating system. There would be men in, he said, with his stare crawling over all my things. I had better be ready, he said, month's time, he said, and then he looked me in the eye and said that I had better clean up this mess.

The television flourished like some fleshy square fruit. We had a few days of false spring, and the sudden warmth in the air seemed to bring it on somehow. The plasticky casing grew skin as thick and soft as a cheek. A bluish translucent layer lay over the screen; the images behind were dull but watchable. I left the plaster on just in case.

When the nights turned frosty again, I woke up at four, and returning to my room after using the loo, I found my television shuddering, very slightly. The tiny hairs on its body were raised, and it was covered all over with goosebumps. I found an extension lead and brought it into bed with me.

After that, I kept my television dressed: I tucked a jumper round it when it sat on the dresser by day. During the night we curled up together, with it whispering stories and the plots of old movies. We went along this way for a week or two; we were happy, my television and I.

One afternoon, I was sitting on my bed with it on my lap whilst I stroked its downy fur when the landlord knocked at the door and came in before I could reply. Spot check, he said, spot check for health and safety. I jumped, of course, and as I rushed to stand up, I stood on the electric flex and dropped the television. It didn't cry out.

The landlord said he was a soft touch, and that he should never have let rooms to DSS tenants. He smiled like a fist and said he was a sucker for a pretty face. He knew his rights within the law, he said, and this place was a fire hazard. There were lots of people out there, people with jobs, who would jump at the chance of a nice affordable bedsit like this. Then his gaze fell on the poor television and he raised his eyes to the ceiling. Proper soft touch, he was, and he said that I might as well forget about my deposit too.

This sort of thing, (at that he pointed violently at my television), this sort of thing would get me more than evicted. That was truly it. He didn't need people like me buggering him about. He was off to speak to his solicitor, and he had a good mind to call the police, bloody mad cow that I was. The landlord left.

I reached down to my television and lifted it like a fallen baby from the floor. Already a bruise was growing along one innocent corner. My poor television. I cradled it to me and rocked it, sobbing. It smiled gently back at me with the face of Carol Vorderman. The landlord would come, or somebody else would come, and I would be homeless and my television left defenceless.

The thought of it was more than I could bear. They'd throw it out, most likely, leave it to die of exposure in some nightmarish landfill. I brushed its poor hurt flank with my cheek as I stood up.

Its weight was awkward to balance when I stooped to pull out the plug. After I straightened up, I could hold it firm against my chest, facing inward for one last embrace. And

32

then I went over to the window, shoving it open one-handed.

When it fell it did not scream, but dropped placidly through thirty feet of air, resigned. My television met the tarmac all in a rush, splattering blood and flesh and fractured casing in a sad and broken splash.

VANITY

THE SKY WAS diagonal with sleet today: slanting and grey, collecting in the hair of the shoppers on Gentlemen's Walk. I was standing, deep inside my coat, watching them push along in jolting streams. One of the shops was belting out Christmas carols on a loudspeaker; it rang against the gritty pavements and came to my ears in an unfamiliar key.

I stood there for the longest time, seeing, until I heard a sound approaching, like the singing of a busker when you turn a corner and come across him sheltering against a wall. It was high and breathless, and sadder than hospitals; when I lifted my chin, I realised that it was coming from the sky.

There, high above me, a seagull was turning in the air and weeping. It was the most beautiful noise that I had ever heard. She was shedding tears too; big sad drops that I could tell weren't the rain because they were hot as bathwater. I felt one drip against my cheek and was astonished; when I lifted my palm to the air, there fell three more. The seagull was choking with sorrow.

I shielded my eyes from the sleet and looked up; her head was black, but the rest of her was bleachy white, and her eyes were bright and blue and thick with lashes. When she saw that I was watching her, she cried the more, until I thought I'd die. I crept through the people until my back was resting against the window of Starbucks. The gull was gliding in spirals, strung up from the sky by Christmas carols and thermal currents.

A man walked past me frowning at his phone; with one hand he held a little girl by the wrist. He was going much too quickly for her, so fast that she was almost falling down with every step. She was wearing little ankle boots and a thick hooded coat, but her fingers were bare and cold and red. The seagull cleared her throat and cried louder still. The man had turned to the child, and shouted at her for dawdling and I couldn't bear to look any more, so I called up to her through the water and the crowds: I called out, Seagull, why are you crying?

Because I am sad, she said, And because I am sick. Because I am going to die and not a soul cares for the death of gulls. At that she wept all the more, with a noise like music, so much louder and realer than the Christmas carols and the angular, elbowing crowd. Someone shoved at me to get past, but it didn't matter, not a bit. A baby started to howl, but it wasn't gorgeous like the weeping of the seagull.

It was so cold on the Gentlemen's Walk, and I felt sad for the sobbing bird, so I called up to her again. I asked her if I could help, if maybe I could ease her anguish a little. Perhaps she would like some chocolate, or just a shoulder on which to cry? At the very least, I had a clean hankie in my coat pocket, but I wasn't quite sure if offering that to her would be polite.

Shedding fat hot tears with every word, the seagull replied that I could never help. She said that my even asking her was cruel, for people were vain and mean and selfish, and as far from God as they could be. Seagulls, she

35

went on, were pure in soul, were almost angels in fact, although cruelly neglected by the world and forced to live in poverty and dine on chicken bones and pizza crusts.

I denied it, of course I did, and I emptied out my purse to prove it. I threw all my dole money to the seagull so that she could buy better food and a warm place to sleep, but the coins fell among all the busy feet of shoppers, and the breeze picked at the fivers and tens. When I lowered my face away from the seagull, they were nowhere to be seen.

The seagull sniffed sadly and said that money was all very well for those who had it but, she said, seagulls were poor in every way. What use is twenty quid, she asked, if you have nothing to your name but wings? For gulls, she said, are identical to each other, and none are uncommon, or beautiful or ugly. The whiteness of gulls is cold, she said; it is just like wearing snow.

I gazed into the heaving crowd, and I saw what the seagull meant: everywhere there were colours of skin and hair, and people who were fat or tall or balding. I looked back up at the seagull with brimming eyes and I told her that it was not because we are proud, just that we are made that way. She laughed at that, and her laugh was as tragic and chiming as her tears, and told me that I would not be parted from my beauty for anyone, and certainly not to cheer up a poor unhappy seagull.

I smarted at that, and as the shop music began to play that song by Slade, I hunted in my handbag for scissors. I waved them at the seagull: they were meant for nails and were small and silver and sharp. I said to that to prove that I cared more for her than beauty I would cut my hair, if she just said the word. The seagull stopped her sobbing for a

36

moment, and the relief was so huge that as I sheared off my hair, I cried myself, with the joy of it.

It took me a long time, as the scissors were so little and my hair quite long, but eventually my hands were full of tangled brown locks. I held them up to the wheeling seagull. I asked her did she want to have it, to weave herself a wig or make a nest with it, but she laughed and told me that the police were coming.

Sure enough there were two men in uniform, pushing slowly through the Christmas shoppers with their radios beeping, heading my way. The seagull flew in curls above my head, laughing and laughing and calling me an idiot, until she gave one last snigger and vanished through a rip in the sky.

SLEEPER

AT THREE O'CLOCK in the morning, Charlotte turns,
half-wakes; the springs of her little bed creak as she
folds her arms and draws her knees up tight. Ward
Nineteen is quiet; in eleven cubicles, people are sleeping.

In the twelfth, a girl is crouched on the floor beside her
bed, smoking a fag, although it's not allowed. Her hair is
waist-length and very tangled. She's pregnant, although she
doesn't know it yet.

Charlotte knows it though, as she sleeps. That babe is
curled like a fern, tiny as a fingertip; it feels Charlotte, feels
her and flicks its little budding limbs. Charlotte's heartbeat
replies like a lullaby.

The girl with tangled hair has bandages on her arms. She
is looking at the floor, where the pattern on the carpet looks
like scattered words. The night is very long; beyond the
walls, the darkness stirs dry leaves by the fire escape.

At four o'clock the atmosphere is thin. Charlotte doesn't
mind; she is dreaming of water, and her dreams bathe Ward
Nineteen in soft, clean air. The girl with tangled hair is in
her bed now, holding her eyes shut by willpower alone. The
babe inside her is thinking secret thoughts; Charlotte hears
them and she smiles.

The dormitory door opens then, impossibly quietly,

spreading white-yellow light along the floors and the curtains that mark out each bed space. The curtains are thick and orange and flame-retardant. A nurse without a uniform slides each one open in turn, peeks at every sleeping face with a pen-torch.

Charlotte feels the light against her eyelids, and her dream deepens. Without struggling, she pushes her back straight and turns onto her stomach. The nurse has a little clot of cancer gathering in her breast; Charlotte chides it, gently, like a misbehaving toddler. It is ashamed then, and begins to melt away. Charlotte sleeps in silence, with her grey hair thick in her face, and her hands spread out, trusting.

At six, the songbirds ask permission. To tell them yes, Charlotte throws out an arm, as if the gesture meant nothing at all; then she unsmoothes a swathe of blanket with her knee. The birds are grateful; they begin to sing.

At six o'clock, the girl with tangled hair is up again, and her face is shiny with crying. With no dressing gown to wear, she gets out of her bed and creeps into the bright corridor.

She hesitates at the nurses' station, then treads the dull floor as far as the smoke room. It is hours until medication. She wonders how she will cope. Charlotte is breathing like the ocean, and knows that she will manage somehow.

Then, all of a sudden, it's seven o'clock, and the winter night might not last forever after all. Charlotte is sleeping still, in her hospital-issue nightshirt, and while she sleeps, her face is uncreased and young and not afraid.

When she sleeps, her bed is warm, and the universe grows a little warmer with it. All this is true: she is all energy and love when she is sleeping, but when Charlotte is awake, she knows nothing of it.

Still, at half past seven, the dawn uncloaks the Drayton High Road and pales the windows of Ward Nineteen. Soon, the dayshift will park their cars in the cold and arrive in their coats and make coffee before the eight o'clock handover. They will talk of last night's telly and bitch about an auxiliary who's still off sick, and the night staff will rub their noses and yawn.

Soon, the curtains will be opened in the dorm, and the bell will ring for breakfast and pills. The people will wake up, frightened, depressed, angry, all trying their best or not at all. They will make Charlotte get out of bed and she will cry and flinch and whisper to herself, but it is only because of her that the earth still revolves on its perfect, crooked axis. It is only because of Charlotte.

WAITING

THE POST IS late on Stanley Avenue; it's where the man who does the Thorpe Road route ends his shift. The post is late, and so is the dawn on winter mornings. The post is late at number 10, where the house has been carved into joints, and every door along the hallway is stopped up with a Yale lock.

The letters flump dryly into a thick wire cage, and the landlady creeps down the stairs like a spider in slippers. She is holding a key, and she turns her wrist to undo the padlock. Then, she stands in hallway, and looks through a sheaf of envelopes. Her husband's gone out for a paper, and he's been ages. She is annoyed.

There's a water bill for the house, and BT quarterlies for each bedsit. She sorts them into little piles along the dresser, one for every room. There's a postcard for her at 10a, from someone called Maria, who's in Cypress and is enjoying the sun. the sea and the you-know-what.

The landlady's lip tautens like elastic, and she flips it to peer at the picture, which is of half-dressed skinny people and water of an unhealthy blue. A colour, the landlady thinks, that you'd find in a bag of sweets. She stands there, frowning, until she comes to a decision; then, she tears the postcard from Maria in two, and tucks the bits into the pocket of her cardigan.

41

The rest of the morning's mail is secured in brown envelopes, and they cannot be investigated even if held up to the light, so the landlady concedes defeat on these, and begins to stuff them into the letter racks screwed side by side on the wall. Two for 10a, one for 10b, five for 10c. (This is excessive, she thinks. Whatever is he up to in there?)

The landlady herself, and her husband, live in 10d, in the attic floor, where the roof slices the wall off into slopes. She patters slowly up the stairs and closes her door quietly, the way she tells her tenants to. She does not slam it; merely closes it, decently, avoiding unreasonable noise, and applies the chain to the inside for security.

Her husband only nipped out for the paper. He is taking forever; she is angry. The landlady goes to his armchair, where there is a cup of coffee on the table, untouched and tepid and growing a milky skin.

She tsks and picks it up; the surface cracks into thin icebergs that float and collide on the liquid's surface. She holds her face tight as she conveys it to the sink, like a radioactive thing held out at arm's length with tongs.

The landlady washes Larry's cup with a tiny drop of Morning Fresh, rinses it, then places it on the draining board, upside-down. Then she stands at the sink with her fingers braced against the bottom of the basin, looking out of the window. Larry is taking his own sweet time.

She will have to go out herself and buy milk, as he's not back yet. Probably, when he does turn up, he'll have bought milk too and they'll have too much to drink and it'll be wasted. The last time she saw him, he was whitefaced and tense, and sweat was rolling down his neck from the pain.

All the nagging she had in her had done no mite of good.

His cough grew more and more, and, although he denied it, he seemed to hurt everywhere: his back, his belly, his legs, even. He did not believe in doctors, butchers the lot of them; and pills stuck against his throat and gave him bellyache.

So, over months, he went away from her; he'd sit inside the fortress of himself, spitting and splitting from pain and fear, and fury at the way in which she went on at him.

Before he nipped out for his paper, she'd heard him beside her in bed; heard him all night, breathing and wincing and muttering curses, lying stiff as a twig all that time. He was up before five; said he was going to get the Mail because they do a good telly supplement. He had taken the car, even though the Esso garage is on the Yarmouth Road, and that's just a matter of yards. He isn't back yet. She tightens her knuckles and steps away to fetch her coat.

The landlady dons her coat like a carapace; the sheepskin makes a better layer than her own skin, which is transparent and thin. Her hair is fine and bluerinsed; the pink curve of her scalp shows right through. She puts her rainhood over her little round head, and fastens it securely beneath her chin. It isn't raining, but there's a nasty wind, so she won't look too peculiar with it on. She needs to have something between herself and the sky. Then, she pulls on her big black shoes, and her calf leather gloves, and she goes out of the door.

As she is tiptoeing downstairs, the door shuts with a bang; the landlady jumps and grips her purse between her two hands, but it isn't Larry. The inner door to 10a smacks just as loudly; it's that insolent girl with a friend called Maria, slamming around as if she owns the place.

The landlady is furious and she arrives on the bottom

43

hallway shaking like a Jack Russell. She hovers outside 10a for a whole five minutes, eavesdropping, smirking and sneering at the careless sounds of feet and kettle, then singing when she puts the radio on. If that foolish woman only knew how awful she sounded, all elephant feet and off-key music. The landlady laughs quietly, and then lets herself out, watching for cyclists on the pavement. She passes a gang of children at the corner of the road; they hoot and jeer at her furious, glaring face.

Larry is still not back when she returns. Four months is an awfully long time to take when you only nipped out for a newspaper. She is livid, but still she sets out both their lunches on the table. It's a nice bit of pork pie, and half a tomato each, and a spoonful of the piccalilli that he especially likes. She begins without him.

Larry is living it up at sea, soothed and softened by the salty waves; and now his body is as supple as kelp, tumour and all. Larry isn't hurting at all, and the little fishes have helped themselves to the gold from his teeth and his Barclaycard.

Larry went all the way to Cromer for his newspaper, and he did the crossword on the pier. And, when he was done, he was done. He folded it up in his coat pocket, and breathed in really hard, noting the pain, reeling with the pain, making his choice through, and with, and because of the pain.

After that, he jumped, and by lucky chance got snaggled with some netting behind one of the huge wooden struts. And there, Larry's happy enough, out of the rain and the lines from crabbers, waving in the tides and waving them out again. He isn't back in time for lunch.

The landlady chews rapidly and thoroughly, and ends her meal with a couple of spearmint Rennies. Larry's plate is by Larry's chair, its glisten and the scent of cured, cooked pork lurking in the living room. She lets in the fresh air to chase it away, hissing and muttering about her wretched useless husband, and she brews two fresh cups of tea.

At half past one, she turns on the television, sound muted, subtitles on, so she can watch, and listen to the tenants at the same time. One stupid woman talks to another stupid woman about postnatal depression, and then the adverts are all about stairlifts.

At two the tenant from number 10a goes out. The landlady can tell it's her by the clatter of her heels, and the time in seconds between the bedsit door closing and the main house door banging shut.

The landlady is delighted; she's sure now, after a week of record-keeping, that she has either left her job or been dismissed from it. Bold as you like, the woman had been coming and going from her house at all hours of the daytime, so she was sure as eggs not working full-time at the Thomas Cook on the high street as she claimed.

The landlady balanced her special notepaper on the arm of her chair, and composed a letter, in which she demanded explanation. If she was in fact jobless, the landlady wanted to know by what means, pray, did she propose to pay the rent, late as it was by a full nine days already? He only went out for a paper. She is furious.

The landlady stands outside 10a once more, letter in hand. Thoughtfully, she tries the handle, but it's locked, of course. The landlady shows her teeth, then stoops to push it under the door. She doesn't want Maria's friend to wait until morning to discover that she has a new letter. She imagines her coming home from the pub, laughing into her mobile phone, then bending on her stilettos to catch the landlady's note from the carpet.

The landlady straightens up, pleased, and wonders where the devil Larry has got to. Without quite meaning to, she goes to the front door to see if he is coming down the road right now. As she is holding it open, and looking, a kid from a garden opposite chucks a conker and it hits the landlady in the glasses. She gives him a look of pure hatred, but he stares her out until she turns to go back inside.

Upstairs, while the kettle's boiling for Larry's chicken gravy, she logs the child's assault in her spiral bound book, with date and time and injuries received, as part of her campaign to get the little monster back into care. Even by bedtime, Larry isn't home.

UNDERPASS

THIS IS THE music of my death: the tunnel-echoes of my breathing, and the rhythmic yap and snarl of a dog. This is the place of my death: the underpass that ducks below the river; the joint between worlds.

I knew they'd come for me. I just turned twenty-six, which is twice thirteen and an evil number. This is a dangerous city; I know this full well. I was always careful not to leave traces for the bad things to follow. I flushed uneaten food down the toilet, and I never gave people eye contact. I burnt till receipts with matches. But the bad things always get you in the end. Although I tried to think quietly, lied when I was asked my name, they get to know the smell of you, and then you're done for. They always want to take you away with them.

The underworld is not as far away as you'd think; it's spread against the city like cellophane: thin, and shiny; transparent. You can hear the sound of horses when you stand by the lifts in the Castle Mall, and women with long white hair can turn into birds if they want to. I've seen it with my own eyes, in the Memorial Gardens, but the police hushed it up, and the *Evening News* wouldn't print my letter.

I hadn't been concentrating today, not enough. The Poundland bags were cutting the palms of my hands with their handles; I'd bought broken biscuits and bubble bath and tights that would ladder in minutes. I'm careful with money; I don't suppose it matters now. I used to have a coffee jar with 20ps in, to save for electric cards, back when I was alive.

He is stalking around me in circles, one way and then doubling back, cutting off three sides of the tunnel. I'm stranded where the underpass splits four ways, turning slowly to face him, my shopping spilled at my feet. He is glossy-black like broken coal and proud as an idol.

I can feel the river above my head: greasy and slow, and somehow beneath some different sky than the one I left outside the underpass. The current drags sideways at your skin. There's only one way he'll let me go, and that is forward, across the water that's surging past the ceiling, and through to where the air is much too thick.

The black dog was a dropped glove in the high street, lying in the gutter and getting wet. I stopped for a moment to pick it up; something about the touch of it, the veiny stitching on its empty palm made me flinch. I looked around for somewhere to put it, and I plonked it on the top of a postbox, grateful to let the thing go. I was careless, gave him my scent. I have only myself to blame.

I glance behind me, just for a second, because the black dog is sitting on his haunches now, and I wonder if I could run, but then he's up and snap-snapping at my face again. I lean away from him and catch my ankle on a Tesco bag; before I know it, I have taken another step backward, one step further across the river. He puts his head on one side and lolls his tongue. The underpass becomes just a little bit less real. I find that I am crying.

The black dog was the cola in a paper cup; it was waiting

48

on the table in McDonald's when I came over with a milk-shake and a doughnut. I knocked it over with the corner of my tray, and it spread darkly over the table as I sat down. I sighed, and got up to fetch a tissue, but when I came back the table was dry.

At first I didn't know that he was a dog. By the Jet garage he was only a shadow, the movement at the corner of your eye that you don't quite resister. Once, he was a threat of hail in the sky; the second time, a baby in a black knitted bonnet; then he was a taxicab, a silhouetted pigeon, and the shadow under a market researcher's eyes.

He is gorgeous as death, and tall as my chest. The inside of his mouth is an anatomical pink, and his teeth are small and blunt, and neat as dentures. He pulls his lip right off them once in a while, and shakes his head to shed a string of drool. He yaps and then snarls again; yaps and snarls.

I thought he was a rat in the car park, or a little cat or something, but by the time I was walking through the mall I knew that he was a dog. He wasn't hiding any more, just loping along, a few feet behind me with his nose low to the floor. The people that I passed didn't seem to notice him: he weaved easily among them and I couldn't get rid of him on the escalator.

On Gentlemen's Walk, he began to herd me, forcing me like some dark shepherd until I met the mouth of the underpass. The road, the grass verges, the noises around me grew vague and metally, like the reflection of a world on polished copper, with only the path in front of me seeming quite there. And then, it dawned on me for the first time: Saint Stephen's Street is the portal to hell.

When I understood this, it was way too late, and he was

49

driving me into the underpass's narrow throat. I was cowering backwards now, staggering past the flower stall with my feet among my plastic bags, concerned only that if I tripped he'd have me by the face. I managed to stop myself where the pathway broke into a crossroads, halfway over the river. That's where I'm standing now.

From the corner of my eye, I saw someone coming: a woman with a little child. I whispered to her for help; she stared at me for just one second, and then she put her head down against her scarf and she turned the buggy round, and hurried back the way she'd come. I called after her, loud as I dared: Please help me, I said to the back of her coat, Please help, because the dog is here and he'll make me cross the river into hell. All I got were the squeaking wheels of the pushchair and dwindling footsteps.

I must have been here all night; daylight is blinding the exit beyond the river. The milk has drained from the plastic bottle that I stood on, the last time that I tripped. I'm tired now, too tired to be frightened. All there is left for me are the rhythmic yap and snarl of a dog and the river, the joint between worlds. This is the place of my death.

COLLAPSE

THIS IS THE end of a world, seen in miniature, played out very slow. This is the moment of collapsing, when possibilities dissolve into what is.

Her chest collapses a little more every time she exhales; she feels the weight of herself, airless; flesh and ribs and emptied lungs. Then, she gasps. The library is turning around her like some complicated experiment; as if every moving, coughing, reacting body is acting out some theory; every one of them just an atom.

The new library is all made out of glass and nerves; the one they made when the old library burned. In the centrally-heated air, she can see the souls of millions of ruined pages; trillions of chittering, fire-eaten words. They pat against the filters like microscopic flies.

The sound is making her nauseous. This is the very worst place to sit and understand the nature of things. Behind her, at the computer desk, a lady has sliced her thumb with the edge of a sheet of paper, and catches a drop of blood in her mouth.

Broken letters are stirring in the atmosphere like tealeaves in water. It's amazing that anyone can breathe. She's thirty feet up, looking through a glass wall at another glass wall, with sky beyond that, and the church of Saint

Peter Mancroft. Between the two is bitty air, and a long drop to the ground floor, and a place where you can get expensive coffee. Everything is new and shiny and hard, but the ground underneath is blackened ash.

There are people everywhere, hundreds of them, talking or leafing through books or sipping espressos. Someone is standing beside the massive glass doors, hissing into a mobile phone. The television station's here, too; one floor up, the walls are frosted and emblazoned with 'BBC'. And there's an angel in the foyer, waiting for somebody.

The man who is about to die can't find his library card. He's at the head of the S-bend queue, and the *zth* of his shoes against the stainproof carpet sets his teeth on edge.

He only slept an hour last night; he's scared about work, whether they'll renew his contract. He's crap at his job, and everyone at the office knows it as well. Some day soon they'll stab his back. As this crosses his mind, his turn comes up at the desk, and he stands in front of the librarian with his book between his knees as he ferrets in his wallet for the card.

Then he finds it and pulls it out, and he is shamefaced and sweating and red, and the librarian says something friendly to him but he isn't listening. He shuffles a few feet along, with his bag and his book and the card in his teeth, and when he's out of the way, he puts the book in the bag and the wallet in his pocket and remembers to breathe.

The man who is going to die sits down on a leather sofa, one floor below the Fiction department. He is so very tired.

When you scatter tiny bits of metal over a magnetic field, the shapes of it unvanish; the particles mark out the pattern of the magnet's force. So it is with the charred and floating letters: their darkness and damage collect on what's invisible; unvanish it.

So here it is, plain for her to see, hovering on unmoving wings, picked out by buzzing, charcoal letters. Its body is more insect than angel, but still, it is grasping a long slender sword in its claws, pointing it at the floor like a plumbline.

And, she is staring, staring at it, trying to blink; it is half as tall as the vast foyer space. It's hanging in the air above the floor; the shoulders and heads of passers-by sweep right through its feet from time to time. The letters knock out of kilter when they do, then they shudder back into place.

Its face is from a renaissance painting, all aquiline nose and perfect, tousled hair and empty eyes. It shifts its grip on the sword a little, stretches out its shoulders. It is real. It turns the beauty of its face upwards, towards her, then back to the issue desk. It can sense her.

The man who is about to die will fall asleep at the wheel of his car. The A11 will be closed for several hours, and it will make the front page of the *Eastern Daily Press*. He will be survived by his mother, and a wife who has been cheating on him. After the initial shock has passed, she will be quite chuffed to get the insurance money.

The man who is about to die fishes for his phone, and finds that the battery has gone. Above his head, the woman in the Fiction department can feel the threading of his arteries and the weight of the coins in his pocket; she's streaming tears for the man who is about to die.

The lady on the helpdesk with the papercut is looking at her carefully, trying to decide if she should ask her if she's okay. And, as she is looking, the crying woman gathers herself to her feet and goes right up to the glass balcony, looking through and down.

The angel is gazing back up at her, curious, but then, the man who is about to die zips up his coat, ties his scarf around his throat. The paramedics will cut this off with scissors in forty-one minutes' time. Heavily, reluctant, he begins to walk. He holds the bridge of his nose in his fingers as he goes; as he crosses the foyer, his head clips the heel of the angel.

Slow and fast as a time-lapsed cloud, the angel turns in the air, marked out by the stammering, skittering words, and it drifts through the wall after the man who is going to die. The letters are stuck against the glass after it has gone. The crying woman stands very quietly and watches them go.

MUSIC

RHODA HAD WOKEN to the sound of singing: far off it was, but insistent, like the drawling of the church organ heard from the market square. Rhoda was not given to music, or the church either, and the ladies of the Sunday school had given her up as lost before she was even in her teens.

Nonetheless, there was music, low and aching, hurting her jaw and making the surface of her coffee tremble. When she removed her hearing aid, it was louder. Rhoda spent a long time ignoring it, frowning at her crossword and trying to make her biro work. After a minute or two of useless scribbling, she *tsked* to herself and put her reading glasses down on her bed.

Rhoda began to search for a new pen, stirring her fingers among the knick-knacks on the dresser and the table. She discovered, as she did so, that the music altered as she moved her head: towards the right, it was fainter, but if she hung her head downwards and a little on the left hand side, it was unmistakeable, heavy and lowering like the music of soil. It upset her a little, shushed against her nerves.

She turned abruptly and heaved open the top drawer. Beneath her underwear and stockings, Rhoda hid her valuables: pens, odd change, Murray mints. They stole from her, the care workers, especially that Tina; they rummaged among her things and they pried into her business.

The previous week, they'd stolen her watch, the silver one with the pretty oval face, the watch that Thomas gave her on their very first Christmas. She'd confronted Tina, accused her outright; these days Rhoda always cried when she was angry, and she hated herself for it. They'd patted her hand like a silly old woman's, and they'd made her tea and sat her in the day room with a box of tissues.

Ten minutes later, Tina came in with a big malicious smile; they'd managed to get an identical watch from somewhere, just to fool her. Rhoda knew they'd taken the real one and sold it; she wanted to rage at them, shout at them, but all that she could do was weep. They'd opened the cabinet in the end, given her a tablet.

Rhoda found another pen and held it close to her face to check that it was real. She'd made a little gouge in its plastic with the scissors; she had done with the whole boxful, so she'd be able to tell if they switched them while she was sleeping. The secret groove was there, sure enough; the pen was truly one of her own, but then she found herself distracted by the music again, by its calm urgency. It was growing sweeter somehow, and stronger too. Rhoda leaned forward to see if the sound was coming from her underwear drawer, but it wasn't. She organised it with care, spreading clothes back over her little hoard, and pushed it shut.

Rhoda rubbed her hands together. Her hands were dry, the palms a little shiny. She'd had to take her ring off last month as it was growing loose. She was worried that she'd lose it, so she'd swaddled it in wrappers and hidden it at the bottom of a bag of toffees. The music was brushing against her skin like paper; she put her hand to her ear in case the music was coming from her body. For just a moment, she thought it was, but no, she was resonating with it, that was all. She thought of sea shells, of the way they whisper about the ocean.

Rhoda turned in circles in the middle of her room, bobbing her head like a blind woman, and followed her ears out of the door. There was nobody in the dayroom and the television was off. There was no music here. It grew stronger in the corridor; a window was open, letting in the fresh air. Rhoda leaned outwards, breathed the drizzle and the traffic and closed her eyes. The window wasn't singing. She stepped back a pace.

She stood for a long time then, and the queer music grew louder still, just a fraction, the way that her wall clock woke her every morning with its flat tick-tock. She felt herself growing younger, more real, as if the chanting of the morning was calling her to some other place, some familiar place.

Suddenly, Rhoda found she knew, and she followed the sound quickly, in case it should lose her. It pulled her along the service corridor, past the laundry room and into the scullery. There was a closet there and it was billowing music in dark, soft waves; utterly compelling, utterly beautiful. Rhoda wiped her brimming eyes and straightened her hair, and shyly began to open the cupboard door, like a child creeping towards the voice of her mother, singing hymns in the safe soft fug of the kitchen.

EPIPHANY

THE NIGHT BUS splits the city lengthwise, leaving ribbons of road that are jumbled with the haunches and elbows of houses. It isn't dark, not among these blinkless, brainless streetlamps.

The night is so hot, and it isn't easy to breathe when you're flashing past the lit and unlit windows, and all those children and tragedies and tiny prayerful hopes, scatter through your head like a strobe light. The night bus can't go any more slowly, surely, because if it does then the tyres'll get all glued up with the shouting and the sleeping and the twenty-four hour TV. My head's spinning; if we speed up I think I might pass out.

We turn a corner, and pass a playing field that has a murdered woman buried in it. She broke her neck in 1981, and oh, she is angry. All she has left to her name are the buckles from her shoes and her bones are singing like a finger against glass. She slips out of earshot in a minute more, and the silence is as vile as the last suck on a lolly stick; I shudder and chew at my nail.

The babies are sleeping in the council estate, with their fists by their ears and their feet tucked against their tummies. A black and brown dog is on its last legs in a kitchen; someone's making cheese on toast and crying.

There is just too much life going past the night bus for

me to process, and we're going so fast, and I wonder if I'm going to scream, but at this moment, the night bus shushes to a halt at an empty stop. It sits quite still, exhaling poisonous fumes, but it can't help it; we're ahead of the timetable so we have to wait here. There are three whole minutes too many.

Below me there's a rat sprinting along a sewer tunnel. She stops abruptly, paused in mid step by a revelation. She has heard the voice of the god of rats, and now she is gazing straight up at the sky.

She's staring past the knotted guts of cables and water pipes; she is staring through the layers of the city: fat and skin and concrete and rainbow-oil in gutters. She's staring, astounded, through all those blinkless brainless streetlamps and the metal skull of the night bus. She is staring right through me, inside my eyes, another sudden prophet, a seer of rats and lives and twenty-four hour TV.

GAS

THE MAN FROM the council smells like dirty bedding, and his hands are soft and white as bread. He'd like to wear a sovereign ring, but is afraid that it might make him ridiculous. It's hot, he's feeling it; he fishes a handkerchief from the pocket of his trousers and mops his face. He's got a face like something skinned; his neck folds over the top of his collar, and it's sore near the button, where the sweat collects.

He missed that patch when he was shaving; this morning I saw him smearing it with Savlon, peering down his nose as he held his chins apart to see the raw bit in the mirror. The man from the council thinks he lives alone, but I quite like drifting through the walls of his house, picking amongst his private things. Sometimes I watch him when he is sleeping, spread out and sweating with the windows open, his arms over his face as if he were being mobbed by birds. He often dreams of falling downstairs.

I know everything there is to know about the man from the council. I can see him right now, but he can't see me. I can watch his lungs as they empty and fill. I'm more clever than the internet, me.

The man from the council's leaning on the jamb of my front door, shading his eyes with his hand and screwing up his face, showing his teeth, which are a browny yellow. He's gazing at the frosted glass, trying to see through it, but it's no use, all he can make out is the dewdrop pattern, and brown cardboard behind it. It's written all over with spells, which are encrypted, of course.

I am nowhere to be seen. In fact, I am lying on my kitchen worktop, serene and completely still, monitoring the universe through nerve-endings at the tips of my fingers. I have become a sort of god, but not one of the nice ones. It's like watching CCTV, except that you can hear and taste and smell. It's like being an atom cloud. It's like being a bomb, exploding in slow-motion. It's like being a danger-ous gas. Mind you don't choke.

The man from the council has a bottle of Diet Coke in his briefcase; it's warm and going flat. He glances behind him for a beat, and crouches to open the catches, laying it down against the floor in case the pens should roll away. He pulls out the bottle and gulps at it, then roots through bits of paper until he finds the sheaf that constitutes My Case; it's quite thick. There's a letter from City Hall that he has to dis-cuss with me. It's terribly important.

He checks the flat number, although he knows it already. He looks toward the stairwell again; his heart has quickened slightly. The thought of me makes him a little afraid. The stairs that I make him dream of are made of poured cement.

There are wet circles on his shirt, but he thinks he'll be okay as long as he keeps his arms down. He tightens his tie, clears his throat and stabs at the doorbell. I pulled the wires out weeks ago; he can't tell if it's ringing or not. When I don't answer after two minutes, he raps his knuckles against the door, where the bone is perilously close to the skin. I do not have the slightest intention of letting him in.

Then he pushes back his sleeve to look at his watch, and wonders what he will have for lunch. He missed breakfast as he's trying to lose some weight. Last month, I stalked him all the way to the hospital, and drifted among molecules in the Cardiology Department, as they told him the bad news. But right now, the man from the council is thinking about fries and cheeseburgers; this makes me laugh.

Norwich City Council is a fine and upstanding body of individuals, who believe with impassioned fervour, that the economy of secure tenancy is based upon exchange. Money for flats; quid pro quo, as it were. This is all very admirable. The man from the council considers himself to be in a position of power; this both saddens him and makes him feel rather important. He has been very forbearing over the months, as he appreciates my difficulties and my complex needs. The man from the council is really very funny.

But now, it has come to a point where there are tough decisions to be made. He plans to say that he must balance my needs against those of my neighbours', who surely have a right to live in their homes in peace.

He's been worried about this meeting, bless him; he woke too early this morning because he was worried. He muttered what he was going to say under his breath as he smoked a cigarette in his car. He is here to help, you see, and eviction needn't be considered as a death sentence in our enlightened age.

For instance, the man from the council knows of a care home, on Silver Road actually, where vulnerable adults like myself can live in little flats of their own, virtually autonomously. There are trained, supportive staff, and in-house assistance with medication and bills and cooking.

I am nowhere near as vulnerable as the man from the council; I can hear the labouring of his heart, the sinewy hinge of its valves. He clatters the letterbox this time, loudly, and then he looks at the sky. It's just about to pour with rain.

I like the spattering rain you get on hot days. When it rains really hard, the sound of it on the stairwell is deafening. The man from the council's glad that there're five more storeys above his head, because at least he's got shelter.

The kitchen counter is narrow, but not as narrow as me. The shiny varnish on the melamine is made of spilt black coffee with sugar, and it sticks against my skin. I tidied all the stuff off it last night, the kettle and all that, as I'll not be needing any of it now; I threw everything off the balcony. I have been lying here for three hours, nine minutes and forty seconds. The gas fire's on in the living room, unlit; the stove too. The hob taps make a rushing sound; a sort of empty hiss.

The man from the council's getting pissed off now. I knew he was coming today; he put a note through the door on Friday, saying that we needed a face to face talk. I read it without even opening the envelope. He looks at the stairwell again, and at the place next door; he hopes they're not in, because if they see him, they'll give him grief for not taking me in hand. They think that I poisoned their dog, and they don't like the presents that I send them through the post. Someone keeps covering their doormat with bits of broken glass.

The man from the council is at his briefcase again, digging out a packet of Lamberts. He lights it with his face to the wall, out of the wind. He had to buy another lighter at the newsagent's, because last night he was going to give up, and he put all his fags and ashtrays out for the dustmen. At that I laugh again, but it sounds more like a dragging sort of cough as it's getting rather hard to breathe.

The man from the council thinks he hears me, laughing and coughing; now he's really quite annoyed. He is certain that I am messing him about. He rattles the letterbox again; he's buggered if he's going to leave, not if I'm inside after all. He takes a long, ravenous drag on his cigarette and tries the door handle. He is surprised to find that it's unlocked: it swings inward easily. The explosion bursts the front window into thousands of tiny, sharp triangles. It's ever so pretty.

VOICE

THE PREACHER STALKS to the corner of the stage, then turns on his heel and comes back again. Listen, the preacher says, to the still, small Voice. Be quiet, he says in a whisper and puts his head on one side. Listen, says the preacher, listen for that Voice, deep in your heart. That Voice, says the preacher, is the Voice of your soul.

I don't want to be here. I don't know why I'm here. Two big men in the High Street were handing out flyers an hour ago. Their eyes sparkled when I stopped for them. They said that Jesus wanted to meet me today.

But all there is here are ranks of locked-together plastic chairs and a preacher who looks like a dead man, and a high, huge rectangle of a room that's freezing with air conditioning. Pastor Tee is visiting for a week-long Gospel Rally. I wonder what they did with the regular pastor.

The preacher raises his arms up in the air and prays so hard and so loud that there are white flecks of spit in the corners of his mouth. God's own rabid man. He is elbowy and grey as suede, and his teeth are false and perfectly white; perfectly even. His hair's white too, and escaping from where it's meant to be; sticking against his forehead, standing up on the back of his head.

I'm watching for his feet and the flex of the microphone. The preacher is marching up and down, but God never lets

65

him trip, not even a little stumble. Repent, says the preacher, for the ways of the flesh; the arrogance of the flesh. Listen, yells the preacher, for the still small Voice that whispers in your very soul, and pleads repentance!

You can see who belongs here, and the people that they have made to come. All the church-women have scarves on their heads; flowered dresses; faces full of earnest tears. Not like me.

The windows are set in the roof; all you can see is heaven. Sunset is turning it gory. There's a life-sized plastic cross screwed to the back wall behind the preacher. It must have bulbs inside; it's glowing like a jellyfish. Part of it is flicking off and on; after a bit, it decides to be on, and stays that way.

They put the lights on as the dusk gets thicker; the cold air's still blowing though and I'm frozen; I'm shivering, or maybe I'm afraid, but then the preacher makes us all stand up. Amazing grace, we sing, that saved a wretch.

There's a piano, some guitars too. A fat man is playing on a drum kit with his eyes closed. The lyrics to sing are plastered against the wall by the cross, written with light from an overhead projector.

The words are written in fussy little capitals and aren't focussed quite right. The projector throws a little rainbow against the ceiling. Perhaps it's a miracle. I feel sick. The people who come here every week are waving their hands; the air above their heads is spiky with fingers.

And then he's saying we must go forward; Come forward, says the preacher, Invite Jesus into your heart; find eternal peace. And he looks right at me, with his eyes as cold and silver as knives, and he opens his arms for sinners to come and be saved.

He steps right off the stage and walks among us; without the microphone his voice is thin and hissy. He stalks along the aisle, stops at each row of chairs, scans every face. I try not to look. There's a lost hairgrip on the hard green carpet, pink and metal-coloured where the pink is flaking off. But then I do look up.

He's like a stage magician, like a hypnotist, like the stranger my mother warned me about; and then I find that the claws in his eyes have gotten hold of me. He swings round on his heel and stomps back toward the stage, and I'm wrenched out of my seat by the eyes.

I'm gasping, sobbing for breath, and I'm on my feet and then I'm sprawled at the preacher's feet, and he says to me that I am saved. He pulls me up to standing, and bellows to the audience of the One Lost Sheep; and they're cooing, cheering gently, praising God. And I stand there at the foot of the stage, held there fast by the claws in the preacher's eyes.

There are more people around me, maybe half a dozen lost sheep, but people are spilling from the front row, putting their hands on our shoulders and backs as if we've won a race. Some of them are crying; the air's too cold to breathe, and the audience is swaying and humming and someone's fainted, but the preacher says God did it.

Then Pastor Tee bursts into the knot of people, hunting out the ones who came forward for their souls' redemption, or because of the claws in the preacher's eyes. The real church people part to let him though, beaming like they're stoned, leaving us pinned like stakes dug in the ground.

And the preacher comes right up to me, closer than a dentist, and he puts his hand on my forehead and it's sweaty, and he barks without his microphone; with his voice splitting from shouting, the preacher barks Be healed!

The crowd that's humming and swaying all gasp at once as though they've been hit or someone scored a goal, and it's all wrong because I don't need healing. And I look at the preacher because if I pull away, the claws in the preacher's eyes will tear my eyes, and he orders me to Be whole but I am whole, I am whole. I was.

I sit down on the floor, very slowly. There's concrete underneath the carpet; I lay my fingers against it, feeling the skinny layers, my white skin against the green, the fingers nicotine-stained and the floor dirty in a line along the foot of the stage, where the cleaner is lazy and missed it with the hoover. There's a woodlouse by my hand, stuck on its back like a tiny dead spaceship. I stay like that.

When it's growing quiet, and the people are shaking hands and embracing each other and putting on their coats, and the ground below the stage is just a growing vacant space, then I hear it. The still, small voice, the one you have to find within yourself, is a sound like an animal choking, coughing and coughing, suffocating, always on the point of death. Now that I can hear it, it never, never stops.

SHOPPING

WHEN I WAS a child I was sent by my mother to the grocer's to pick up the tins and dry goods for the month. With an ancient pushchair that I was to use as a trolley, and the hood of my coat pulled over my hair, I scurried down a sidestreet, the wheels racketing along loud enough to wake the dead.

When I saw the grocer's ahead in the dark, the light and warmth from it made me think of illness. The shopkeeper was standing in the doorway; I slowed right down and walked towards him reluctantly, half deafened by my awful pushchair. When I stopped in front of him, the silence whistled in my ears like a milkfloat. The shopping list was clenched inside my hand; I took one step forward.

The shopkeeper held the door for me; I ducked beneath his arm and entered the shop. Inside it smelled of mothballs and tobacco and cough candy. Boiled sweeties were lined up in heavy jars along the top shelf; a butterfly wing was plastered to a flap of flypaper.

The shopkeeper lifted the hinge on the counter and folded himself behind it, wiping his hands on his apron. With a flick of his headmaster smile, he asked what he could do for such a sweet young lady out all by herself in this weather.

I glanced behind me, at the grocer's name spelled out

backwards in the window, and the plastic crates laid out beneath, filled with potatoes, cabbages, carrots. A flayed brown curve of onion skin lay by itself on the floor like half a secret message. I put my fingers in my mouth.

The shopkeeper was standing there, beaming encouragement. I took the shopping list from my fist, and uncrumpled it carefully, running the creases with my fingers until it was almost flat; I laid it out as lightly as I could against the shopkeeper's palm. His hand sprang shut.

A movement caught my eye, and I strained my gaze sideways as he read the list aloud. Tea. Sugar. Matches. Abruptly, the shopkeeper swung around and turned his back to fetch and weigh out tea leaves.

A mouse tiptoed out of the shadows from behind a sack of dog food. He was shaking his clever whiskers through the air and against the floor, until all of a sudden he sat up on his haunches with his eyes as bright as spilled jam.

Safety or pink? enquired the shopkeeper. I blinked at him, confused. In one hand he held up a box of matches, Scissors brand; between the fingers of the other were Swan Vestas. Pink, not safety. I pointed. He laid out an oblong tower on the counter: four, five, six. The seventh one unbalanced the lot and they toppled with a rattle. The shopkeeper turned away again, humming.

In the very corner of the shop was a mousetrap, garnished with a dried-out twist of chicken skin. The mouse rubbed his paws against his nose and began to groom his fur, wiping the ladles of his ears. The shopkeeper trundled a stepladder through from beyond the door frame. The bead curtain was made of plastic lozenges threaded on strings. Three long strands were tangled together. Climbing up a step, the shopkeeper reached up for soap. Bars of Lux were wrapped up in twos.

The mouse sat up again; the creaking of the ladder had upset him, and for a minute he froze quite still. If noticed, he was hoping to be mistaken for a toy mouse. The shopkeeper had my mother's list in his hand again and he was holding it out at arm's length, frowning. He asked me if by soda she meant baking or washing. I didn't understand, and he was smiling much too much. I shook my head and stared at the grazes in the counter's varnish. Some were quite fresh and others were filled in with dirt. The shopkeeper laughed and my eyes filled with tears.

The mouse was looking right at me now, nodding his face up and down. I think that he was telling me something, but he was very small so I couldn't quite hear. Then he found a little crumb on the floor and he held it with both hands, tasting. The shopkeeper said that I had better ask my mother about the soda and that he didn't have the cheap tinned tomatoes, so would Princes do? I nodded, not looking up. The mouse had found that his crumb was soap powder, and he put it sadly down.

The shopkeeper rummaged under the counter for a box; he found a thick brown square like one that had been squashed flat. I watched him from under my eyebrows as he turned it from a killed box to a real box, with wide parcel tape that sounded like ripping when he stretched it out from the roll. The mouse had turned his twiddly tail towards me; he was smelling at the air again.

There were heavy sounds as the shopkeeper stacked tin cans at the bottom of the box. He left the ant powder and the tea for the very top. I couldn't see the things go in because the box was tall and the counter quite high. The shopkeeper started saying that I had better button my coat right up because it was starting to rain and I didn't want to catch a chill, did I? My nose was runny and I didn't have a hanky so I used the back of my hand. The mouse had gone into the corner where the trap was. I stared at him ever so hard but he didn't catch my eye.

Then the shopkeeper said Three pounds twenty, please, and wasn't the cost of everything so much these days? When I was your age, the shopkeeper said, but he didn't finish what he was saying and just laughed instead. I took out my mother's purse and found four pound notes. When I handed them to the shopkeeper he said that I was a Good Girl. The mouse had crept right up to the trap and he was thinking, Goodness me, what's this great big thing, and I knew that I had to get out exactly there and then.

I shoved the change in the purse as fast as I could, hopped from foot to foot while I waited for him to write out the receipt. I tried to slide the box towards me, but the shopkeeper said, Let me get that, it's heavy and he carried it over to the pushchair and sat it there like a great square baby. Then the shopkeeper put his hand at my face and there was a shiny boiled sweet inside. That's for your trouble miss, he said, smiling like a rocking horse. I knew the poor mouse was about to die so made myself look him in the eye, and I said Thank you very much.

After that I fled into the drizzle, with the thundering of my pushchair as loud as when a train goes straight through the station and doesn't stop.

NIGHTMARE

THE NIGHTMARE BEGAN in the cupboard under the sink, where it twitched in the dampness and blinked its embryonic eyes. By February, the thick air had turned its gills to lungs, and it whined in the dark. When the summer warmed the kitchen, it quickened its stupid heart.

One day it heard you singing as you sat at the table with your crayons, and fell ruinously in love. Thereafter, it listened for you, learned your voice with sightless devotion. It smelled the dinners cooking, and memorised your chatter. When you ran up the stairs, it counted out the footsteps.

One awful day you grazed your knees, and it sobbed and sobbed all night. Then it wiped its greasy tears with the membrane of its wing and vowed devotion beyond death. The first winter slowed it, but still it grew beneath the sink trap, swaddled with j-cloths and a rag of tissue, chanting Christmas carols.

During 1982, it chewed right through the rotten chipboard at the cupboard's back. For weeks, it picked its fingernails between the lino and the wall. Now it was hungry and oh, so sad; it rocked on its haunches and yammered like air-locked water pipes. It was cold, and no one cared for it, not even you.

Three years later, it despaired, resolved to contemplate the question of itself. It sat and ground its orange teeth, hunched and bitter like a cake of laundry soap. Wedged between the floor brushes and the rat bait, mummified it was, and hardly real. In sleep it smelled of mice and damp. When it dreamed, it dreamed of you watching TV with the light off. The tiny hairs that line its ears can hear your very nerves.

Now just you wait. One day you will go back to that house and stand in that airless kitchen. And when you hum a song that you recall from long ago, your nightmare will shake its sticky muzzle and crawl shyly out to meet you.

BLADE

ANYONE WOULD THINK that the knife had come off worst, the way that it tracked me like a puppy dog, followed me around like Mary's Little Bloody Lamb. Overnight, everything that had happened became a dream, unreal and nasty and in slow motion. I had taken it upstairs with me, a magic talisman, so that if my dad came, it would be the last time, for sure.

When I woke, it was there, on the floor beside my bed, streaky with red like some prop in a cheap DVD. I snatched it up, and wrapped it up in toilet paper, and stuck it in the wastepaper basket in the bathroom. Halfway through my breakfast, I thought of it there, and I heaved with a mouthful of cornflakes. I managed to swallow it, but only just; I left the bowl unfinished, and my mother shouted at me for wasting food.

She was in a mood because He had gone again, just like that. My mother's eyes were narrow as glass; he'd taken the housekeeping with him, I could tell by simply looking. I went to the toilet and washed my face; when I opened the cabinet, the first-aid kit fell out like an empty green clamshell, and all the things that belonged in it fell after. The roll of bandage was missing, the scissors too, and there were brown thumbprints over everything. I tidied it up and pulled the zip right round. Then I got out my toothbrush and cleaned my teeth.

At lunchtime I told a dinnerlady that I had a headache, and asked if I could sit in the Library Corner for a bit. We're allowed indoors by ourselves, now that we're in the top year. I'm almost eleven, after all. She said had I eaten my lunch already, and I said, Yes, but I hadn't really. Then one of the little ones came over, streaming tears; she'd fallen flat on the playground and filled her hands with gritty blood. She seemed like a baby to me, like a silly little girl. We're all too old for crying now. The dinner lady started towards her, so I tiptoed carefully away.

The knife was waiting for me there, patient, but eager somehow. Seeing it made my head feel light and heavy at the same time, like a balloon with a weight in it. I didn't have any tissues this time; in the end I got my gym top out and picked it up with that. I could feel its sharpness through the fabric, the way that the white cotton stuck to its bloody backbone. I flinched, shuddered through as far as the floor, and shoved it behind the bookshelves.

Then I saw that it had left a slimy red-black trail behind it, as if it had crawled all the way to school like a slug. I kicked and scuffed at the shiny floor with the toe of my shoe, like my brother does when he tips fagash on the rug at home. My mother cuffs his head when he does, but he always does it anyway. I scuffed in lines until the marks were all rubbed in. Back in the Library Corner, there was a thick stain on the carpet where it had lain.

It wouldn't come out, not even when I spat on the sleeve of my jumper and rubbed at it with that. Anywhere else in the classroom it wouldn't have shown up, but here the floor was soft and mauve, with cushions on it, and a comfy chair as well.

Then I had a good idea, and I got out one of the drawing pastels that I got from my Nan at Christmas, and I put it on top of the bloody mark and trod on it. It was just fine; all the powdery bits completely hid what was underneath. I scraped up the mess as best I could with the sides of my hands, and then all you could see was chalk dust.

After I washed my hands it was still in my fingerprints, all gathered in the little skin creases, marking each tiny line orange. When the teacher saw the carpet and shouted at us, I put my hand up and said that it was me, and that I was truly sorry. That shut him up. I was put on litter duty at afternoon break, but that was okay.

On the bus I caught it digging a split in the seat, dragging out the hairy stuffing with its blade. I shoved it in my bag but I found that it had carved my name in the plastic handrail. By the time I got off, it had put sticky smears all over my English book. I rubbed at the stains with my finger; it smelled like money, or the bars of the climbing frame in the park. Luckily we had to cover all our exercise books with shiny fablon stuff. Maybe it's in case we got blood on them. I felt sick again at the thought. I dumped the knife in someone's front garden and wiped my fingers on my skirt.

I don't like going home much. School is a pain, in a way, but I do like learning things, even though the other kids say I'm Keen. That's an insult, but I don't care, because I like reading; it makes you forget where you are. My favourite word is Sanguine: it is cheerful, and calm; it shushes like the ocean, or the tiny rustle of burning that you hear when you draw on a cigarette. I'm not keen really; I just like forgetting where I am.

I stayed out as long as I could, walking around, looking

in shop windows, until it got so cold I had to go to my house. A light was on in the hallway, and I knew He must have come back. My mum wouldn't be there; she doesn't finish work until nine. They open late on a Wednesday, you see, so she has a long shift. It's just me on Wednesdays; I'm supposed to get my own tea.

I dithered for a bit; finally I decided to wait outside and watch. The knife was there already, shiny and sly on the low wall. I sat down next to it, wishing that I'd nicked a smoke off my mum before I left for school.

He was in there; I could feel his sweat and the bristles on his chin. I sat, wondering what to do. After a little while, the door opened, but I didn't flinch. My dad came out with a holdall on his shoulder; he was limping really badly, gripping the muscle of his thigh.

I looked at him, silent; he glanced at me sideways, and the knife slithered towards me, protective. I heard the metal scrape of it against the bricks. He didn't say a word, just struggled off down Lothian Street with his bag. I stood up very slowly, looking at the open door, and then back at the sticky knife. Then I took it indoors.

LISTEN

THE ONLY PERFECT silence in the world is at the centre of perfect noise: the still point in a hurricane, or the core of you when you have been pushed so far that you're reamed right out. That's when you are completely calm. The nicest noises are unbroken, rhythmic or continuous; torrential raining or road drills. If the noise is complete, it doesn't matter where you are, because nothing can touch you; not even the chicken factory, the feathers and the blood. You're safe, inside noise.

It's only when you can't hear yourself scream that you can find the microscopic prickle of your nerves, and nothing, nothing, else. That's where the quiet hides. Then, you are aware of the silences inside yourself: the soft rhythms of blood and oxygen and carbon dioxide.

There is noise in sleep, when it's good sleep. The best dreams are deafening; the very worst are made of tiny sounds, half-heard: heavy topplings and the hollow sounds of breaking. The worst kind of dreams makes me thrash my bedsheets into twisted ropes and buck my body, 'til I make a space between my bed and the wall.

I just got my final warning, typed and printed and in a brown envelope. I opened it there and then; I had to strip off a latex glove with my teeth, with the supervisor leaning over his desk, both of us standing. I'm holding one screwed-up inside-out glove and one mucky still-on glove, and the envelope is under my arm and I'm trying to read it really quickly and my forehead is welling up with sweat.

There's a noise that fills your mouth when you know you're going to faint: a noise like the buzzing of a moth when it's trapped between the lampshade and the bulb. I hear that, for just a moment, but it fades and I'm okay after all.

The supervisor is an alright bloke; he's sorry, he really is, but it's his neck on the line, I must see that. At that, he waves his arm at the door, towards the shopfloor, at the chickens swaying along the conveyor, and he snips his fingers across his throat like a mechanical blade. Then he lets out a weak hahaha that rolls over the table like ball bearings before it spills away.

Rules are rules, you see, and they are imposed with good reason. The supervisor is staring at me, flicking from one of my eyes to the other one and back again, as if he's trying to figure out if I am listening carefully. I am staring back.

If he was to let me get away with this one breach, they'd all be at it. Before long, the safeguards will have all gone to buggery and they'll end up closing us down when some daft sod loses a hand. Or goes deaf. And it's the likes of him who'd catch it then.

The supervisor has a point. The factory is noisy, and it is a matter of common sense that you should wear ear defenders when you're at the machines. But I like noise. I need noise.

When I was a kid there were noises in my house; late-night noises from the kitchen. They used to burrow into my dreams; muffled thuds and voices too, Spitting Image caricatures of people that I knew. There'd be my mother's voice, or something like it, but the high tones hard and shrill, and my father low and dangerous like a nail in a carpet.

By the morning I might easily have dreamed it. My mother would be just the same as herself. She'd be there like always, smoking in the kitchen, looking at her lap, as if there were something sitting on it, invisible or impossibly small. My dad would throw back his coffee like vodka before snatching up his keys. He would kiss the top of her head then, and she'd carry on looking at her lap 'til the front door slammed.

I like the factory in a way, at least, I don't hate it the way that some of them do. The first day, everything smells really bad, but by the third you don't notice it any more. All there are is layers and layers of sound. The noise is so perfect that I can put up with the mess, no problem.

The last night that I spent at home did not end in head-kissing. I lay awake for a long time, trying not to hear my parents' puppet show voices; then there was a huge sound, like a table falling sideways, and a high, seagull crying. I put my hands over my ears, but I could still hear it with my fingernails.

You know what's what with the factory; the noise is massive and flat and perfectly safe. Sighs, swearing, the sound of your feet: against the machines and the birds and the clattering it's all as good as silenced. You could sing at the top of your voice if you took a mind to. My eviserator's like a vacuum cleaner; when they're slaughtered and scalded and all that stuff, the chickens come round to me, all still dangling by their feet. I have to put the hose in and suck out what's inside.

After that big crash downstairs, I knew I'd never get to sleep, so instead I stood up; my legs were shaking like a newborn kitten's. I only wanted to close the door, but I ended up creeping downstairs; I discovered myself outside the kitchen. I didn't want to, but somehow I did. There, on naked feet, I stood, listening; not wanting to listen.

There was an open, flattish sound, like a frying steak slapped against a worktop, and my mother's voice, almost; raw like bones, bloody, incoherent. She sounded like a barking dog.

After that, there was a bellow and a crash, and a different sort of crash. Then I heard the oddest thing, a wet, hollow thumping, as if she was pounding bread dough with a rolling pin, and sobbing at the same time; one thump, one sob. There was thumping and sobbing, over and over; she thumped and sobbed as I ran up the stairs and wrapped myself in my duvet and wedged myself lengthways in the space between my bed and the wall.

I didn't see my mum after that, not at the funeral, not even after they let her out of prison. The judge was very sympathetic; she only got twelve months, and was out after nine.

At the machines you don't have to talk, there'd be no point if you did anyway, and I'm a good little worker; efficient; clockwork-quick. The supervisor thinks I'm an example to others my age, if only I'd stick to the rules and wear my bloody ear-defenders. My social worker says I am a star, and she reckons I'll have my own flat by the time I'm eighteen.

But when you wear ear defenders, it ruins everything. You sound like the bottom of the swimming pool; the space inside your skull gets jammed up with echoes and the sound of knocking. The silence gets in your ears first, and then it gets in your sinuses and your lungs, and the pressure and the knocking fills you up like inhaled Vaseline, and you know it might just kill you.

So here I am, looking up at the supervisor, and he smiles, so I smile too, sort of, and I take off my other glove to shake his hand. He looks at me the way a teacher might; with his face all creased from smiling, he tells me to run along, now. Then, suddenly, he reaches forward again, and takes the ear-defenders from around my neck, where I'm wearing them like Walkman headphones, and he puts them on my ears with another hahaha, only this time I haha too, just a little bit. And then I'm off, back to the eviserator, with my head filling up with echoes and pressure and half-heard thumping.

DEMON

I DON'T GO in bins as a rule. I have my pride, after all.
Even so, you do spot things from time to time that it'd
be a sin to waste. When I was doing my rounds yesterday,
I did find a real treasure, or that was how it looked. I'd been
doing a spot of tidying up before the light went; found a
really nice trolley in the Safeway car park. Its wheels were
good; that's the main thing with trolleys. Some kids had
already prised out the pound coin, but it had a separate
compartment where you can put your valuables and things.

There wasn't anyone around, so I pushed it round the
back, all casual like, and when I'd hidden it up nicely I went
to get my old trolley. There was a dirty great seagull sitting
in it when I came over, picking with his great big beak at all
my lovely things. They're born thieves, birds: crows are
always after my tinfoil and the golden paper from Benson
and Hedges boxes, and the gulls are forever trying to rob
away my dinner. I shooed him off, but he'd already nabbed
a slice of bread out of my Homepride bag.

I love tidying up. In half an hour I had all my treasures
organised in layers with plastic bags in between. I had thirteen Coke cans that had been squashed by cars; they're
beautiful when they're flat; I could run my hands over their
contours for a month. I had more then twenty blue things,
including one baby shoe that had been lost by someone and

found by someone else. When I came across it, it was spiked up in the rain on a black set of railings, blue and wet and gorgeous.

By the back doors of the supermarket, where the bakery is and they put out the rubbish, there's always bin bags, lovely strong black ones. My plastic top sheet was a bit tatty, so I went to get some from him who works in the storeroom. He's a good boy, calls me Miss, he does, and he gives me my bags, and sometimes stuff that's going out of date. Not that I beg, you understand; I am not a case for anyone's charity. I thanked him very gravely with a slight bow, and I'm just tucking them over the top of my trolley when I spot something shiny on top of a heaped up wheelie bin.

There wasn't anyone to see, so I went to have a proper look. It was a half-bottle of whisky, that's what I thought at first glance, anyway. So I tucked it into my big coat pocket and pushed my lovely new tidy trolley up towards the high street. It was a lucky day for sure, because I found two ice lolly sticks with jokes on them (different ones) and it turned out that my nice alcove was empty.

Recently, my alcove has been stolen sometimes, by nasty swearing kids with scabby arms, who sit and whine for spare change from anyone walking past and shout at each other. They sneer and call me grandma. No respect. It's a lovely alcove, raised up on a step, with its own street lamp, nicely out of the wind and with a pretty view of the jeweller's.

After I'd settled myself with my blankets and my Bible, I took the bottle out to have a proper look. The seal was still intact, and it was full right up with something golden, like whisky or brandy, or maybe rum. It was one of those that's got two flat sides, and there was no label, which was odd.

Now I'm no drinker, you understand, not with how it ruined my old mum, but it was a pretty thing, this bottle. Its shape made me think of a round bottle that's got left in the sun and gone gooey, 'til the sides sank flat. There was something though, like a tangle of threads within the liquid, that gave me a pause. I found my glasses inside my bag of things made of glass, and I held it up to the streetlight.

At the centre of a fragile web of blood vessels was a tiny knot of something living, something that had a huge blue eye and a little throbbing heart in its middle. I was surprised, in a way, but then I thought, well everything has got a life of a sort, hasn't it?

I watched it for ages, pulsing in its network of bubbles and nerves; after half an hour I realised that it was growing, slow but visible like the minute hand on a clock. Delicate mauve buds developed and began to become limbs, and a tiny squashy face began to pick itself out of the softness.

Before I knew it, it was kicking out time at the pub over the road, so I thought I had better keep myself a low profile. It was getting a bit on the nippy side, and I was worried about the baby, so I put the bottle inside my clothes and pretended to be asleep until all the laughter and shouts had died away.

There's a sound to the night, the proper night, between the last of the drunks and the security guards walking home at five with sleep in their eyes. In the proper night it's so quiet you can hear the wind stirring litter and the creaking of the hanging signs of shops. In the proper night, tomcats maraud in the gardens and people have their throats cut whilst they're sleeping.

I dozed a bit, until the proper night woke me up. Inside my cardigan there were two rhythms now: the stubborn beat of my chest and the hopeful flutter of the baby. When I took the bottle out, it occupied half of the space inside; it had developed stubby wings, studded with the itchy points of sprouting feathers. When it saw me, it began to drum its little hooves. I put my thumb against the glass, and it trailed its miniature fingers against the inside of the bottle where I had touched.

I ate some of my bread whilst I watched the baby forming. It grew, quicker and more quickly now; its eyes darkened to a chocolate brown, and it learned to blink at half past three. Sunlight was straining the dark by a quarter to five as the baby heaved its wings against the sides of the bottle; by now they were longer than its body and stuck at a painful angle against the corner.

It had grown a fragile pelt, fine as suede and a bluish white, and its silvery hooves were sharp and precise as a lamb's. A cloud of hair, the colour of whisky, had gathered over its head by six, and it began to tap on the glass and mouth words to me. I put my ear against it, but all I could hear were bubbles.

I feared for that baby's life by seven; it was crushed by the bottle on all sides. I asked, by way of dumb show, if it wanted me to break the bottle, and it nodded. So, even though it's a sin to break glass, I broke it. The poor thing flinched with every blow; on the third knock against the ground it shattered and the baby was sprawled and gasping in a bright sea of splinters. I picked it up and dried it on my cardigan, flicking off as much broken glass as I could.

After that, we looked at each other for a long time,

almost embarrassed, whilst the baby's wings dried out and unbent in the air. The girls who worked the tills at the Safeway's were coming into work in ones and twos by the time the baby tried to fly.

It couldn't; the wings would heave at the air, and it'd almost lift, but the chubby baby body was just a tiny bit too heavy. I've seen it before with swifts that end up grounded; they can swoop and soar, but only when they're helped into the wind. So I picked it up, weighed it in my hand for a moment, and threw it away as hard as I could.

That did the trick. It spread its feathers and filled them with sky. After a moment of fluttering it began to glide, and finally it turned in the air and flapped slowly away without looking back. I watched it go, and finally gathered up my blankets and started to tidy up my trolley. By ten I was off on my rounds, and wanted to look in at the Day Centre because Jo said that she'd get me a new coat. It wasn't until dusk that I arrived back at my alcove.

When I did I was a bit surprised. All over the step were a heap of blue things, so many that I found myself getting to my knees before it, amazed. There was a flower, a blue plastic one like something plucked out a cheap straw hat. There was a blue stripe ripped from a Tesco bag. There was a broken string from a necklace with four lapis beads still threaded on. There was a glassy chunk smashed out from the blue light on an ambulance, and a shred of blue cloth from a nightshirt. On this last was a drying smear of blood.

WITNESS

I DON'T SLEEP well. At the Elim House you get a key for your room, and they get your Housing Benefit, and that's about it. There's a bathroom between each dozen of you; there's no plug in the sink and you have to stop it up with loo roll. I wouldn't touch that scummy bath with a barge-pole. There's a kitchen, as if anyone was together enough to cook; we're all the Not-Quite people, here. Any worse, they'd not let us stay, but if we were any more alive than we are, we wouldn't be able to bear it. Or maybe we're just that bit too alive, too aware; skinless.

Leon next door, he's a junkie; he keeps it low key, else they'd throw him out. There's a girl at the end of the corridor, who I think is called Helen; well, she's on the game, but as long as she doesn't bring anyone here, it's okay. Most of us are just normal: we do our best and wait for our Giro every other Tuesday.

My CPN suggested this place to me; I've been here ages now. It's worst at night, it all gets inside your nerves: if you hold your breath and listen there's the sound of fifty lives all jammed together, all off-key and clashing like a child banging on a piano. Tonight, most of them were sleeping: four or five were dreaming, one thought he was falling and he screamed and screamed inside his head.

Fourteen others were awake and having sex or worrying

about this or that. Some girl I didn't know was jacking up, I felt the needle go in her leg slantwise and I felt sick. There was someone else, someone old, who was just breathing, in and out like it was the hardest thing that he could ever be made to do.

And that was just the people. The Elim House was so, so sad; it'd stood there on Jamaica street for one hundred and thirty-nine years. It'd been built to be the local workhouse, then they made it shops and after that, offices. In the eighties, it squatted on the pavement, empty and dark, for months.

It feared for its life back then, with its windows knocked out one by one and the flashing nicked off its poor aching roof. School kids played with matches in the superintendent's office, 'til a smackhead with a flick knife scared them off. It had nightmares of fire, the old workhouse, where it saw its floors sunk inwards like a corpse's eyes, and the woodwork blistered as far as the bone.

And then the church folk bought it and it became Elim House, with a manager in the superintendent's office who said he'd pray with you, and singing on Sunday evenings in the television room with fag burns on the lino.

After that, the old workhouse, the Elim House, just sat there, dumb and fazed and depressed, and full of people who swap their Housing Benefit for keys to their own rooms. It isn't bad here, better than the night shelter: nobody's violent and no one has ever died, except that boy last year, but that was meningitis.

The girl I didn't know had crashed out with the syringe still dug in her flesh; its cold sharpness bit my thigh every time I tensed my leg. She was so faint that for a while I was really scared for her. When I found her mind out there in the dark, she imagined she was running with horses, whilst a long thin line of blood trickled over her ankle.

At two, I gave up and stuffed my laundry bag. There are always lights on at the all-night laundrette on King's Road. I go there when everything gets on top of me.

I put my Walkman on before I pulled the big security door shut; I always play white noise when I'm feeling a bit anxy. There's a point between radio stations where the static makes a sound like water. It's lovely. I put my bumbag right down in the bottom of the dirty washing in case I got mugged. I always carry pound coins and twenties for the dryers, and then plasters and aspirins as well. I like to leave them around, on the machine that vends soap powder, and in the library, and on the bus, wherever people might get hurt.

I've had mothers shout at me sometimes, as if I was trying to poison their kids or something, but I'm actually helping, not hurting anyone (I always cut the aspirin packets up, and leave two at a time, in case someone who's depressed tries to overdose).

My CPN says I'll get into trouble one of these days; he's tried really hard to scare me out of it. But what if there's someone out there who's hurt and who's in pain and she needed plasters and aspirin at exactly that moment, but there was nobody in the city who cared for her enough to have anticipated her need? Then, it'd be my fault. I would have let her down, and made her suffer. I would be no better than a torturer.

I turned my noise right up and started to walk as hard as I could through the night. It was freezing outside, the air misting with drizzle that was cold enough to hurt your face. By the time I turned into King's Road I was almost going at a run, waiting for the moment when you are warm enough with walking to not feel the cold.

When I got to the door of the launderette's I stood at the window and looked inside. I'm no fool; I'm not going to get myself shut in with some psychopath, but it was empty. So when I got inside and shut the door it was like heaven, only smelling of fabric conditioner and still air. Sometimes when I go to the laundrette I wish I could ease my self into the dryer and set it going, and gently rock my body in lovely warm circles.

Well, anyway, I took all my washing and shoved it into the machine, and then I posted in the money, and the water started to flow in with a clunk and a hiss. I took off my coat and spread it over two of the seats to dry, and then I began to turn the volume down on my radio, gradually, so the silence wasn't a shock.

There wasn't anyone nearby: no breathing or snoring or talking, not even the cynical brown rats below the floor. After a couple of minutes I took the headphones off, and then I felt a quiet so sharp and grating it made me wrap my arms around my chest and suck my teeth. The launderette on the King's Road was still as catatonia; it daren't even rock, but knelt on its foundations unblinking and speechless.

I realised that I was thirsty, and cold too; now the novelty of being out of the wind had worn off, my wet hair and the unheated room had caught up with me. I was thirsty and I was cold and the laundrette was utterly terrified. I went over to the washer and rested my cheek on its top. It was slightly warm, and the rhythmic vibrations from the moving drum were soothing, in a way, until it clicked into spin and I felt the building jump.

Sometimes I just get sick of all the pain there is in the world. You can worry so much about everyone and everything that it makes you ill. Last summer I swiped a wasp with a magazine when he kept trying to climb over my face, and the ghost of a wasp kept me awake for weeks afterwards. After a moment's annoyance comes guilt, you see, every time. I sighed, more tired than anyone has ever been, and I went back outside to find out what was the matter with the laundrette.

King's Road was astounded; without my radio, I felt it the moment I stepped onto the pavement. It was horrified, trembling like a flat concrete leaf. A police van drove past me, dead slow, and I saw a fox who flashed her eyes from behind a road grit bin, but apart from that I was alone. Every tread of my feet made the road side flinch, although I was trying to go gently, and it was getting worse the further along the road I went. The jittering pavement was driving me nuts, and I was miserable as I turned the corner into Franklyn Street.

At the back of the laundrette, even the streetlights were hissing. I found it hard to catch my breath as I stood and saw. Something awful had happened; all there was left in the road were thick black tyre streaks and a million glittering cubes of windscreen glass. I couldn't bear the sight of them, so beautiful in the streetlamps, and so perfect. On impulse, I knelt down and picked one up. It was blunt and green, and when I held it up to my eye, it was opaque.

That poor, poor road. I had no plaster big enough, and

any number of aspirins wouldn't have done any good. Instead, I lay down, cheek to cheek with the asphalt, spread out my arms and cuddled it as best I could. For an hour I smoothed it with my fingers, shushing it like a huge flat child, until Franklyn Street and I both fell asleep in the dark.

LOVE

ONCE UPON A time there was a little old woman, who lived in her council flat, and was as lonely as lonely could be. She had been retired from her old job at Superdrug when her hearing seemed to be on the wane. She had accepted her glass clock meekly, and the last-day paper cup of fizzy wine, then cried on the bus all the way home.

Still, things had not been entirely hopeless. Sitting in front of the television one afternoon, she was dawdling aimlessly through memories of childhood, when a thought occurred. As a young girl, she had been thoroughly schooled in domestic matters by her grandmother: cooking, of course, but there was also crochet, dressmaking, embroidery; she could probably even make lace if only she had a good think. Her grandmother had said to her often that there were few jobs more honourable than that of Mother or Seamstress.

She decided, therefore, to be henceforth a seamstress, the gentle craft of motherhood having cruelly eluded her a long time ago. She put an ad in the *Evening News*: The Seamstress, her adverts said, Garments Made to Specification, Wedding Gowns a Speciality. After one or two false starts, including one episode when she somehow mistook centimetre measurements for inches, her life took on a new shape. In three months, one could not move in her bedroom for the fairy-wings of sewing pattern that lay in fragile layers over the floors. The carpets and the chairs were strewn with delicate snipped-off threads of cotton; pairs of sewing scissors lurked like metal crocodiles under innocent folds of silk.

The seamstress would not tolerate the notion of machine sewing; this earned her a certain reputation, and indeed a following, amongst customers from quite far afield. Thus was her pension supplemented, and she sat in her rocking chair every morning with her needlework and an angle poise lamp. All the while she was as sad as ever, and alone in the world.

One night she lay in her bed, unable to sleep for the humidity in the air, whilst above her roof the sky gathered together the energy to shout. Quick as a gasp, the rain began, and juddered the street so hard that car alarms began to squeal up and down the blocks of flats. It was then, she recalled later, exactly then that she resolved to make for herself a son. And, with this idea firmly planted in her soul, the seamstress turned onto her side and slept right through the clatter of the storm.

The following morning the seamstress was woken by the swearing of the dustmen, and she climbed out of bed and started work without even stopping to make a cup of tea. By four o'clock the sun had moved to the back of the flat and she *tsked* at the dwindling of the light; only then it dawned on her that here she was in her nightie, thirsty and with her fingers aching from gripping the scissors and the needle.

After brushing her teeth and making herself a sandwich, she took a very deep breath and returned to consider what she had made. It was good, as far as it went: a neat wee body with two feet, two hands, and a stuffed bag where a head would sit. The seamstress thought to herself, What a silly old thing I am, reduced to comforting myself with toys.

With a mournful wag of her head, the seamstress began to cry, and she held the raggy thing close. Then a small voice, muffled by her shoulder said, Mama, why do I have no face? Well, the seamstress jumped, and her heart was filled with fear and hope. She swept the table clear with her arm, sending cotton reels, pin cushion and a half-made bridal gown flying, and then, with a tiny, frightened smile, she reached into the drifts of cutting patterns, and she padded the wooden surface with a scrunchy paper bed, and put the little creature gently down.

The seamstress unplugged the telephone and stood for a moment at the window. Now the kids were back from school, a noisy game of football was underway; boys of seven and eight chased each other along the pavements, all the while cussing each other like navvies. She gazed at them, eyes overflowing, and closed the curtains in case of spies.

The seamstress upended her paper bags of fabric odd-ments and made for her boy a beautiful patchwork face from scraps of leather, with the softest chamois for his lips and ruddy oxblood cheeks. Mama, said he when it was done, Mama, why do I have no eyes? And the seamstress bit her lip and thought. Reaching for her button box, she picked out a pair; plastic they were, and shiny-black. After stitching them in place, she found tiny ivory buttons meant for the sleeve of a wedding dress, and she put a row of pearly teeth into her new son's mouth. When he blinked for her and smiled she was the happiest old lady in all of King's Lynn.

The day that followed was bright and perfect, too involved in mother's love for the seamstress to be bothered with answering the door when the girl called round for her dress. Together they chose the clothes he was to wear, and the seamstress made them for him while he gazed in wonder at the deftness of her needle and thread.

She made him a little hat, as he hadn't any hair, and as she fitted it on, he said, Mama, what is my name? Ah, she replied, you are Boy, my boy. Boy, he repeated slowly. And then he looked up at her again, and said, Mama, I am hungry.

Now this made the seamstress stop and frown. For a long time she stood silent with creases over her face, until her Boy piped up again, Mama, what can I eat? She sat down on a heaped-up armchair, and lifted her Boy onto her lap and asked him what he would like to eat. He just shook his head and said that he didn't know.

She went into the kitchenette and made him beans on toast, and sat him at the breakfast bar. But at the first bite, he shuddered and said to her, Mama, that is not food. The seamstress turned her cupboards out, and gave him bread and jam, and cheese and tea, and fish fingers, and frozen pizza. She even tried dry Cup-a-Soup but the poor little waif could eat none of it.

That night she went to bed with her Boy wrapped in blankets next to her; he put his tiny velveteen hand against her cheek and fell asleep.

By the next morning, the seamstress had had an idea. She sat her Boy at the breakfast bar again, but this time she presented him with a plate of fabric scraps. Mama, he said, this is skin! She gave him a bowl of kapok, but he began to cry, saying that she wanted him to eat guts. She was sorry, she said, over and over. He keened his hunger all day and all the next week. The neighbours rang the doorbell from time to time; once or twice, people shouted to her through the letterbox.

The Boy the seamstress made grew thin as if his stuffing was ebbing out. Their days grew desperate with love; each knew that there was hardly time to waste with breathing; there was so much love to spend that the flat grew wretched with it.

Mama, said the little thing at last, I am nearly dead. Mama, he said, I love you. And the poor seamstress cried and apologised and loved the poor wee thing until he starved to death at last. Everyone said after that, that she was a queer old fish, carting around that funny little rag doll, all wrapped up in scraps of lace and satin.

COUNTING

ONE IS FOR my dolly, who watches the house with her face a perfect zero. Her name is Christine, and her eyes won't close anymore. One is for the tiny cup of Ribena that they make you swallow at Children's Communion.

One is for our house, which is small and square, and wears its textured wallpaper like blankets. One is for the staircase with a carved acorn on the last banister, big as my knee when I fold my leg. One is for the lollipop that the ambulance man gave me, flat and round and wrapped in plastic. It's turning to glue on my windowsill; I bent its stalk trying to lever it off the gloss paint.

One is for my dressing gown cord, made out of plaited colours like a pigtail; but then, I don't have it any more, so perhaps it's a nothing after all. One is for the pigeon's wing I found in the street, stiff and the colour of mucky snow. The bird was nowhere to be seen, just the wing she'd left behind, and a reddish raggy bit where it should have joined her body.

One is for my Nana, and one is for my Mum, and one is for me as well. My Nan used look at my Mum sometimes, like she'd recognised someone in the street, someone wonderful, but then she'd realised it wasn't the wonderful person after all. Or as if she'd been given a present to unwrap, but it had only had a new school blouse inside. Then she'd stalk off, out into the garden, even though there hadn't been a row. My Mum would be left there in the kitchen, staring at the slammed door, with her fingers all filthy from peeling sack potatoes.

I have two shoes, scuffy and buckled, and my feet skip the rope, one-two. They're patent leather, and the shine is cracking along the line where I bend my toes. We had two cats before, but my Mum took Calico to the vets in a cardboard box. Now we've just got Marmalade, but he scratches if I try to pick him up. Two is for my eyes, which are green and sprinkled with chips of brown, and two is for my Mum's eyes, which are green as well.

When I saw my Nan, I thought she was playing some queer game. She was dangling, with her feet above the seventh step, as if she was planning to jump out at me and say, Boo! Her skin was like purple chalk, and she was pulling the rudest, funniest face that she could think of. At first, I laughed, and squeezed past her on the stairs, to see what was holding her up. She had borrowed my dressing gown cord; it was tied to the handrail at the top, where it fits round the hole of the stairs like a wooden cage. The knot was very tight; much tighter than shoelaces.

There are three important people in the entire world: my Mum, my Nan and me. I don't see my Nan now, but we have to hold her in our hearts instead. There are three kinds of sweets that I like best: cola bottles, and cough candy, and space dust, which pops against your tongue, and nearly hurts but doesn't quite. Three is for the Trinity; the Holy Ghost looks a bit like a blue nightgown, floating in mid-air without anyone in it.

When I told her to stop, she just ignored me, even when I asked her nicely, so I sat down on the carpet to wait until she got bored. She didn't. It was ages until my Mum came home from the shops.

Four is a clapping game: Salt, Pepper, Vinegar, Mustard! Four is the number of my bedroom walls, where the paint's the colour of luncheon meat. There are four long knives, stuck in the block in the kitchen. They're made out of Sheffield Steel, and I'm not allowed to play with them.

When the ambulance pulled up, they rang the bell four times, but my Mum didn't even blink at the sound, just stood there in the hallway, facing the wall, holding the phone. She was making shapes with her mouth as if she was practising for a spelling test; the phone was making that woo-woo noise that it does if it's been left off the hook. It sounded like a tiny ambulance, calling to the big one outside.

Then they hammered on the door, really hard, and my Mum flinched and dropped the receiver. It dangled on its twirly wire, not quite touching the floor.

When I hold my breath I can count a slow five before I find that I am beginning to die. Then, my head bursts up from the bath water all in a rush, half-blinded by soap and delighted and panicky, all at the same time.

PROCESSION

THEY CAME TO Mrs Hope at dusk. The message was for her alone, although plain enough for anyone to have seen it: in the middle of the weather forecast, the girl said that a new front was coming. Coming, she repeated, and she looked right through the screen at Mrs Hope, to make sure that they understood one another.

Mrs Hope understood, and she gathered up her knitting and placed it in a careful pile upon the round table. She brushed her grey straight hair without looking in the mirror, and when she opened the front door, a tiny wisp of night air curled its way down the hall.

As Mrs Hope walked, her way was guided by a vibration, a distant thrumming that pulsed through the street like the beating of horses' hooves. After a minute or two, she leant against a wall and eased off her shoes so that she should be able to feel it better; at any rate, they made her feet hurt. Mrs Hope's ankles were swollen and thick, and the poor hot flesh was not used to the cool of the outdoors at night. Her tights thinned to holes beneath her toes as she went along the cold dry road.

The shopping mall was open late on a Tuesday, but by half past six it was very quiet. Mrs Hope stood on the escalator with her mind as open as the huge sweeping thoroughfares. The drumming carried her around to the left, until she stopped beside the lifts opposite the Post Office. There, in nodding streams beside the metal shutters, the horses were dancing for her.

She stood there for a long time as the horses processed through the Castle Mall. As she stood, with the Christmas lights reflecting on her skin, it dawned on Mrs Hope that her entire life had only been preparation. This was a curious thought, in a way; one might have thought it negated everything that came before, but Mrs Hope knew that nothing whatever had been a waste.

Not a second, not her childhood colouring books, not Eric, not her job at the shoe factory, not her long patient years of motherhood, not even the sudden graveside or the horrified silence of the living room, not one bit, she knew now, not one bit had been in vain. Everything narrowed: the whole of life had been sharpening, growing smaller and more precise around her, so as to meet in a point at the moment in which she was called to stand before a procession of horses.

They appeared from nowhere, as if they stepped right out of the solid wall, and they pranced and pawed for miles until they were invisibly small. Somehow, the thirty feet between the Post Office and the HMV encompassed the distances between planets. The hollow clop of their hooves and the snorting, blowing sounds that they made, filled up the Castle Mall like steam and made the fine hairs on Mrs Hope's temple stick down against her skin.

They slowed as they passed her, tossing their heads and moving their mossy-soft lips as though whispering some equine language. They gaped and rolled their eyes, as though they could not quite believe her, as if they wanted to press her into their memories, to be sure.

They passed her by the thousand, calm reserved mares with gawky foals, and arrogant, headstrong stallions that showed off to her about their sweaty flanks and the arches of their necks. Mrs Hope nodded to every one, knew each to be perfect. They passed her by the thousand, and they did not stop when the cleaners came out of the service door with a floor polisher. Then, suddenly, a tall palomino drew to a stop and stood, anxious and stamping.

Mrs Hope hesitated for just one moment, looked behind her as the tannoy announced that they were closing. Then she placed her flat hand against that horse's side and felt the realness of him: his sweat and odour and the great slow thud of his heart. After that, Mrs Hope and the horse began their journey.

SUNSET

WHEN THE SUN didn't rise, I slept late until I was thick-headed and sluggish. I finally woke when my mother came into the room and stood beside my bed. She said nothing, just stared at her wrist until I rubbed my face and rolled out of bed. The carpet was thin under my feet, and the air was oddly cold. I put on my dressing gown.

My mother had been awake for a while; I sat at the table while the kettle boiled, holding the kitchen clock in my hands. My mother had taken it from the wall when I came downstairs. She held it out to me, shoved it forward, asked me the time.

It said twenty to three. I was confused, wondered how long I'd slept. I shook the clock, held it to my ear; its slow tick was calm as stones. I stood up and went to fetch my watch from beside the sink; it patiently read the time as two forty-one.

After that, I collected every clock we had in the house and brought them to the table, where my mother sat and sipped at her tea. Even the ugly little watch that my grandmother had worn as a ring all declared that it was before three.

We went to the back door and forced the sticky catch; behind the pear tree the sky was the colour of a sore eye. There was almost no light; just enough to pick out the blade-tips of the grass and the starlings in silhouette on the fence. I put my hand in my mother's and leaned against her

106

side. My head came up to the top of her ribcage. She didn't move. I pulled my mother's hand over my head so her arm was around my shoulders. She still didn't move.

The hours drooled along until it should have been evening. I waited for my mother to cook, but she just wanted to sit at the table and watch the garden through the window, so in the end I stole three biscuits and a slice from the cheese. When it should have been night, I pulled at her elbow, tried to make her get up to go to bed, but she wouldn't. I didn't sleep much.

Life lost its shape. The house grew cold, although it was still August. The grass in the garden turned the queer white of things that live in caves and my mother sleepwalked between rooms as if she were hardly alive. I eked out the food in the cupboards; I was forbidden from using the stove. Once I did try, but I gave myself such a scare with the fierce blue fire of it that I daren't touch it after that.

The longer that the sun stayed unrisen, the less colour there was in the world. The cherry tree's leaves became ghosts of leaves and the garden began to starve. The lights in our house started to attract the miserable creatures that lived outside, as if they thought I might have some trick to save them.

A robin beat itself to death against the window, like a huge, bleeding moth. Starlings scraped their feet on the glass panes, and a fox with a broken tail barked and shrieked outside the door for hours at a time. Once, he tried to force himself through the letterbox. He failed, but I was badly frightened.

When the larder contained nothing more than cough sweets and a bottle of vinegar, I tried to take charge. I took my mother's purse from her handbag and put on her heavy overcoat. It trailed along the floor as I opened a big umbrella, with which I hoped to protect myself from the animals.

I got no further than the front door; the moment it was opened the air was full of wings and beaks and the murderous claws of cats. I forced them away as best I could with my tattering umbrella, and heaved the door shut. I was not a cruel child; they only wanted to be in the light; they wanted the light so badly. From the living room window I could see what was left of my attempt to go shopping: there were feathers and corpses and black splashes of blood. Hundreds of eyes flashed from the flower borders and the lane beyond. I sat on the floor and cried.

It was the bulb in the kitchen that blew first. There was a fizz, and then that was that. I fled the darkness and went to sit in the bathroom. I tried to make my mother come too, but when the light vanished she just closed her eyes and wouldn't open them. I had to leave her. My mother had discovered the bright place behind her eyelids, and she had gone to live there. I couldn't really blame her.

The lights began to wear out, one by one. I didn't eat for weeks; I grew past hunger, bundled up inside my jumpers. After an age, I began to wish for a crisis: anything to force things towards an end. One mad hour, when the clocks all read two fifty, I ran from room to room upstairs, high with despair and laughing, and I smashed the lights out with my umbrella. When I came to myself again, a pile of time later, I couldn't believe what I had done.

So it was that I came to the living room and stood beneath its fragile, hissing bulb, looking out past the curtains at the white garden crowded with creatures that wanted just to die in the light. I looked at all their faces and at the sore, sunless sky, and, bracing myself, I opened the window for them.

NIGHTSWIMMING

I STOOD AT the hallway mirror, memorising my face, trying to discern some hint of a coming change. Sure enough, there I was, thin as a prophet, a woman made of papier mâché, the skin terribly dry and aching to be shed. I brushed my hair: one hundred careful strokes. I pushed the fringe away from my eyes; my hair would never be bound again. The hallway held its breath and watched.

After that, I stepped from room to room like an exorcist: I made my old bed, wound up my alarm clock and turned the pillow. I bolted the tiny window and closed the patchwork curtains, so no corner of the night could peep through; after that I started the fire.

In my mother's room I lined up the lavender bags from the top drawer; they looked like murdered kittens tied up in muslin. I snipped their ribbons with the nail scissors and spread them flat. I looked in the wardrobe and counted the coats and stroked the fox fur, although it was well beyond saving. The catch caught with a metal snick. After that, I started the fire.

When I came down the stairs I was as coy as a bride. I lit the pyres that balanced at the base of every straight-backed banister. The flames were pretty.

The kitchen was ready for burning, after all those sorry years; I let the stove fulfil its secret ambition. The tea towels were bandage-dry, and the table would go up too, but that would take a long time.

Up the step and along the hall; I stopped at the mirror and saw myself with a smoky halo, listened to the talking of the fire. I opened the piano stool and laid a blaze among the sheet music. I fed it doilies, one by one, until it was too hot to see.

I closed the front door softly, so as not to wake any poor old ghosts. The windows held swirling mists of smoke, but the alarm might not be raised for an hour. With this thought, I unbuckled my wristwatch and posted it through the letterbox. My hands were black, but they wouldn't stay dirty for long.

It wasn't far to the river. I gazed at its calm green depths and jumped with a graceless tangle of legs. It was cold, my it was cold. I kicked and clawed at the surface, gasping and flailing at the moon. I got a last skew-eyed glimpse of the blackness of sky and one heartless star, and then, thank god, it changed.

There is a moment where violence becomes beauty; when you fill your lungs with water, you become a fish. My face was washed clean, and the clanging of water became a call, a message from the place that I was seeking. I opened my eyes, and, now that they would never close again, I saw everything plainly. There is perfection in the world after all. My hair was drifting weed when I struck out towards the sea, and my T-shirt billowed as I swam.

It was a long journey, it took me weeks, until the sudden bite of salt made all the seas of all the earth a single, open space: a garden.

When the water grew warm, I felt the music; felt it with

111

my tongue before my ears. There are voices within the ebbing of the ocean, sweeter than brine, and there's light between the fishes' tails. I didn't have a passport, so I showed them how to make a fox's silhouette with my hands.

Our city is small and our dwellings modest; we dig the coral sand with our fingers and we make castles. We weave our dresses from the latticed fronds of kelp. We are happy.

CUTPURSE

FEAR AND POWER are very nearly the same thing. When I am afraid, I am untethered, and I whip in the wind. When I think that you night catch me out, I'm strung as high as heroin. And I'm a dangerous secret; bleach in a lemonade bottle.

I love to steal. I love the suspense of it, and also the tenderness; to pick pockets one must be as attentive as a doctor. It is a kind of love.

Stolen chocolate is toxic. So is stolen money; it coats the skin like chicken fat. So is a baby's feeder cup of juice, eased out of the pushchair when the mother's looking at the label on a tin can and the baby's staring at me.

So is the fingernail I've clipped from your hand, whilst you're sleeping on the late-night train from Liverpool Street. All that's here are you and me, and the lights in the window from houses, and rows and rows of empty seats. Your fingernail is polished, pear-drop red and manicured, and the curve of it bows slightly under the pressure of my hand. These things are gorgeous, gorgeous poison. These things make me happy.

My beginnings were small, tentative as childish experiments often are, but prophetic and magical also. I learned my own religion; discovered my true form. One day before school, in the spring of 1986, in the town where I used to live, every street on the estate was named for a tree: Cedar Drive; Maple Walk; Holly Road. For all my life I was a little girl, compliant, obedient, mediocre; I was barely there at all. I tried too hard; I was rolled with puppy fat.

Then, that morning in April, as the sun shone brightly on my skin like lemon squash, I was walking past the rank that we used to call The Top Shops. The idea struck me like an instruction from God, sharp like a fork on a dinner plate. Half reluctant, as if following some new calling, I slunk into the newsagents and stole a bar of chocolate. Nonchalant and trembling, I walked out of the shop as steadily as I could, thinking my skin might burst outwards from the pressure. Ten yards down the road, I ran.

That day I took the chocolate was vivid and painful; I found myself real in a way that I had never been before. I cried for an hour and a half, until the Mars bar in my fist turned to squitch. When I split the wrapper with my teeth it was soft and warm and luscious, raw somehow. I devoured it; I felt it become some extra part of me: a new internal organ, perhaps, or a modification of the blood; rendering it thicker, darker; sweeter; like the cheap ruby port that I nicked from the caretaker's cubby the next week. That wine was rich enough to make you sick, unless your blood was accustomed to it. Mine took to it readily enough. That first theft made me powerful; that day, I roared with it. And that first night, I slept for thirteen hours; slept like the drugged, dreaming of nothing.

My grades improved; my teachers began to administer house points, and called me Shelly instead of Michelle. They put it down to a blossoming maturity; my dad bought me a brand new bike, and I went to a proper hairdresser's for a feather cut.

I even began to attend a youth group at the church, where I palmed little palm-leafed crosses, and silver coins from the collection plate. In my bedroom, my possessions accrued, catalogued in little finicky lists, wrapped in pale blue Kleenex.

Still, as time went on these things became easy. I stole purses from shopping bags; trinkets from the Christian Bookshop. After a while, I felt that I needed something new.

Stealing a dog was a piece of cake. It was a horrible little thing, fluffy and shaved in places, with a tongue like a drippy scarf. Some old dear unclipped it from its lead when I was sitting in the park, thinking about cutlery, about my shoe boxful of spoons. I scooped it up as it came yapping past me, holding it by the face in case it should try to bite.

I sat for a couple of hours inside a hedge, wondering what to do with my haul, whist the biddy walked up and down past me, calling, Pippin? Here boy! I didn't care, but neither did I want a dog, and then the revelation struck that I didn't have to want the thing I stole any more; I didn't even need to keep it. This knowledge made me stronger yet.

When the calling for the dog grew angry, then pleading, and finally died out altogether, I came out of hiding with it. Now that I was on my feet, it began to struggle again, wrestling its short little backbone against the line of my forearm.

I took it to the duck pond's muddy lip, and I threw it as hard as I could, then shaded my eyes and watched it paddle all the way back to dry land, as far away from me as possible.

And, as my maturity did blossom, I grew to understand the intimacy of thieving, the kindness. A pickpocket is a lover, reaching deep inside the beloved, slipping inside coat or ribcage, drawing out jewellery or fragile fragments of lung.

One beautiful day, I took my scissors to town with me. In the Post Office, the queue for tellers reached right along the mall, as far as the lifts. The people stood there, single-file, sighing, and easing their weight from one foot to another.

The woman in front of me tossed her head and sent a handful of hair flicking over her shoulder. It was long and blonde and very straight. I edged towards her, indecently close. She smelled of shampoo and cigarette smoke. She stepped backwards, careless, oblivious, and I jumped out of the way, quick as a flame. She did not notice. I crept forwards again, smelling the shampoo and the smoke, so ghastly with power and with fear that any moment I might burst out laughing. My scissors were as stealthy as me; I sheared off one lock and wrapped it in a leather glove. When my turn came up at the tills, I bought stamps, and then I tiptoed home.

Which brings me to now, watching you sleeping on the Intercity, in an empty, clanking carriage, waiting for the train to terminate. I'm as quiet as a knife, and I'm frightened and I am powerful, next to you on a table seat, loving as a mother, with ten little red half-moons lined up beside your blunted fingers. And, I'm sitting here, with my long-nosed silver scissors, wondering what else I'd like to take from you.

PASSING

THEY PICK HER up whenever they come across her; the police patrols all know her by name. They call her Lorna as if she was a little child, and then they telephone her daughter and they take her home.

They tell her that the streets are not safe, that she will catch her death with all this wandering. Her daughter says, what is she expected to do? She can hardly lock her in; what if there was a fire? This happens frequently now, more so as she grows older, as if an elderly lady out all by herself at night is against some unspoken law. Lorna's insomnia is her secret talent.

They make her sound aimless, as if she simply drifts along the streets. Lorna does not wander, and she is never aimless, although she rarely speaks any more. People misunderstand her silence, her calm, closed face and her faint smile. She has simply said enough already and she has nothing more to add. These days, Lorna prefers to listen.

Lorna loves the dark, and the city when it rains, because these are the moments when the world belongs to her, is solely in her care. They have not picked her up tonight. Her daughter and her grandchild, and her daughter's thin, resentful husband, are all sleeping, in bed and cradle, and none of them can hear the rain.

It's February and it's a Monday, and although the air is

streaming, and although it is terribly cold, there is hope within the drizzling water, hints of the ending of winter. Lorna does not shiver, but her headscarf is wet right through.

At City Hall, the clock shows four, and the pavements shimmer orange with the street lights. Lorna stands on the steps, between two bronze lions, and looks down the curve of the hill, at the market's coloured hoods. She can feel a death coming.

Lorna's the last of the wise women: a midwife to feral cats, and neck-wringer of injured things. She will not brush her hair, and her coat is from a jumble sale; it is army-surplus green. A fox comes to greet her, politely flattening her ears, and just as quick, she is off; scuttling along the gutters with her brush streaming behind her. Lorna could not hope to keep up, but the fox knows that she will follow.

During the night, the city breathes out, exhales the grief, the traffic fumes and the missed red lights, and it fills its potholes and pores with cold still air. At night, the little gods creep out from building sites and alleyways, timorous as they sniff at the ground. They lope the streets when they're empty, and they trust no human alive but Lorna.

At night, Lorna does not need her spectacles. She gazes through the rain, as the vixen moves like a slip of shine on the tarmac, vanishing at last down Goat Lane. Then, smiling, she pulls the hem of her nightie straight and buttons her coat over it. Thus made presentable, she starts to walk.

The god of Pottergate Green is not big and had never been powerful, not even when people believed in it. Now, it's worshipped only by the foxes, the way that pigeons worship the sky. Tonight, it will die. It guarded the little grassy triangle between the Pottergate Tavern and the chip shop, a wide-eyed witness to shoppers and drunks and pigeons.

Last summer it saw a boy jag a knife at a smelly old man, long after the pubs had emptied. It hid among the bins until the footsteps died away, and then it lay down beside the victim as his life dropped away through a hole in his side.

It comforted him as best it could, nuzzling his face with its great hot tongue, purring anxiously, licking away the sweat and blood, until finally the man's eyes glazed, unshut. When the heartbeat became quiet, and the sun began to rise, it left the body for the police and the world of men; and its sleep crawled all day with nightmares. It has been a skinny life, and tortuously long, and the timid god of Pottergate is finally, for the first time, not afraid.

Lorna pauses at the lip of the road; the rain is dwindling, and the street is very large when it's empty. A couple more foxes have joined her now; her motley little entourage grows by twos and ones as they pass the Guildhall.

Down Dove Street, the silence is growing in the air like crystals; the foxes hate it, and they're straining their huge kite ears, but there's no sound at all but the slow, slow breathing of the city, and the feet and the drip and pat of raining. They bear left at the joke shop, where a reeking litter bin marks the corner. There's a dropped five pound note lying in a puddle, folded in the wet like cloth. Lorna does not pick it up, but sees where it has fallen and nods her head.

The little gods have hidden in the back streets, and they're chewing at their claws, or else worrying at fleas. When there's one god less, there will be a vacuum to fill, one more territory to stretch between them. They do not want more pavement space, none of them do. They're outmoded now and nobody needs them. They do not understand tarmac, or fire engines, or empty plastic packets. The intelligence of people and their quick harsh voices confuse them.

Then, suddenly, there's a car engine, easing its way up Dove Street, slowly because it isn't meant for cars. It's the police, off on business of their own, unless Lorna's daughter has gone to her room to check she's still in bed. Against the night, the intrusion is brutal, almost blasphemous. When the squad car has gone, Lorna and the foxes step out of a doorway and discover that they're almost there.

There are dozens of foxes, every one from every street, all come to pay their respects and to mourn; even the yawning, quivering puppies from by the Salvation Army. They are very sad.

The little god of Pottergate is sheltering against the wall of the pub, splayed on its side, toiling away with thousand-year old lungs. When it sees Lorna, it tries to rise, half rolls onto its front paws, unfurls the ragged banner of its wings. Its tongue lolls with the effort.

It is albino, like a little panther with pinkish, mouseish eyes, and its wings were once long and sharp as a seagull's. It's the size of a dog or a half-grown sheep, and its paws are huge and dirty and soft. Its pelt's like an old white carpet, threaded and ruined and left out for the dustmen.

And Lorna, midwife to feral cats, kneels stiffly on the sodden ground, and she draws her legs to the side until she is sitting next to the creature. She lifts its head, and rests it with care upon her lap. Taking the scarf from her head, and twisting out a handful of water from it, she dabs at the crusts around the little god's eyes, and cleans the foam from its mouth.

After that, she just sits there, stroking the god behind its ears, where the fur's as soft as suede, watching over the little god of Pottergate for hours, until at last it dies in her arms, gently, the way that the darkness slips into dawn on February nights.

BRIDE

MISS LIDDELL WAS riding on the bus. The one that came past her flat had been full of kids headed for their schools in the city; they'd jeered at her from the long seat at the back, called her names. Rude names. Miss Liddell endured this patiently, day after day; she sat calmly behind the driver's booth, with her hands folded upon her lap, and her back perfectly straight.

The sun was vague, and the morning was pale, greyly opalescent and blessed with light drizzle. This very morning, this one, was the perfect morning for a marriage, as was every morning before it. Miss Liddell was a lady most favoured among women. She smiled like an angel until the bus arrived at her stop.

Miss Liddell stood still at the kerbside, smoothing her nightdress straight, adjusting the lace at collar and cuff, and gazing with love upon the people of the earth. She swept precisely through the shoppers, past Monsoon and onto Gentleman's Walk. She stopped at a shop window, and knelt before it to consider her reflection.

Miss Liddell's hair was long and straight and thin, and the ivory-white of bones. A plastic Alice band kept it off her face; with her slender fingers, she plaited it all the way down her back, leaving the end untied. Her eyes were clear but brown; the Creator's gift of imperfection, that she might retain humility.

The people on the market knew her by sight; the man on the haberdasher's called out a rough Good Morning. He beckoned her over and placed an off-cut of net curtain upon her head. The woman at the meat stall shouted at him; with foul language, she called him cruel. The butcher woman was jealous. Miss Liddell secured her veil with her alice-band, and curtsied gravely. The man on the haberdasher's was destined for Heaven, but it wasn't her place to tell him so.

Instead, she turned right and began her beautiful journey through the city, gathering occasional scattered feathers from the tarmac. These were left for her by night by the Groom and His entourage; the bouquet, renewed every dawn, that the Bride might be ever more exquisite than the day before.

She arranged them as they came, slate-blue and white, and held them by their pointed stems in her left hand. The right contained her Bible, with a ribbon for its bookmark, held forever at the Book of Revelations. A white satin purse was looped over the crook of her elbow. Two hours later, Miss Liddell had a lavish swathe of feathers; a fan behind which she might coyly hide.

Miss Liddell processed the length of Magdalen Street in memory of the purified whore; Miss Liddell, too, broke perfume jars, but her soul was already quite, quite pure. She wept a little as she walked, shedding great round rolling tears of pity and compassion for the world. Miss Liddell made no attempt to wipe them; she simply let them fall upon the pearl buttons of her wedding dress. At the flyover, she turned again and retraced the way that she had come.

Between the river and the playground, the Groom had left His wedding ring for the Bride to find. Miss Liddell placed her bouquet on the ground with care, and sat with her Bible upon her lap. It was flattish, and not a comfortable fit; the ring for this day was from a Coke can. It still bore the leaf-shaped piece that once had sealed the drink; Miss Liddell twisted the metal leaf in her hands until it came away. The ring was a little sharp, and had drawn blood from Miss Liddell's fingertip; this was as it should be.

It was almost noon before Miss Liddell returned to the city centre to meet her Beloved. They didn't let her in anymore at St Peter Mancroft, but even so, she stole inside the gate and placed a kiss upon the front door. It was of no matter; she knew that her Groom was not within the church anyway. He was waiting for her now, calling her to Him.

Miss Liddell's heart was white and playful as a lamb as she skipped into the memorial garden. The Holy Spirit burst around her in the form of pigeons as she danced in a circle between their perfect wings, singing, as there was no organ music.

LOUD

I T'S QUIETER IN the smoke room. The carpet's thin and
filthy with fag ash, and the emulsion above the skirting
board is scuffed where it's been kicked. The radiators are
both on high and the curtains are shut. Madeleine creeps
inside the door, and then stands there, holding her hands
out in front of her, poised like birds.

A pair of shoes clatters down the corridor, and then more
slowly there's the pat of bare feet. Someone's laughing.
Madeleine turns carefully, looks behind her. The door is
propped open with a fire extinguisher, and the escape sign
is half picked off and faded yellow.

There's nobody else in here; it's suppertime, but the tinny
scraping and the voices and the brittle air all cut with forks
were just too violent, and so she tiptoed away. She folds her
hands across her throat and sinks her chin to the space
behind her thumb, considering her next move. Madeleine's
neck is soft and loose as kidskin, and her wedding ring bites
a circle into the flesh of her finger. She is wearing a cardie in
girlish pink; the meds have made her fat, so it pinches underneath the arms and the buttons gape.

There's a chair close by. Madeleine places her slippers forward, one at a time, silent and wary, and then she sinks into
it, wincing at the shade of orange and the noisy whispers of
creasing fabric and chair-springs. She tucks herself into a

neat square, feet together, cotton dress spread evenly over her knees.

The clock's gone wrong; it's flicking its second hand against a single point with a tiny and insistent battering. It's like somebody punching a door from very far away, heard through the wrong end of a telescope. There's a shout from the dining room, someone's yelling, just for a moment, and then it all goes quiet. Madeleine closes her eyes and shudders. There's a ten-second pause, awful and howling, and then the scrape of spoons.

There's a dog-end on top of the television, poised there like a clue, balanced on its tip. The burned out fur of ash is perfectly fragile, and the gold band where the filter begins has just charred through. The walls flicker with the coloured lights of a gameshow, but the sound, thank god, is turned right down.

When Madeleine has spread her fingers over her face, and brushed her skin all over, just to check, and when she's sure that the ponytail is keeping her hair tied back, she looks over to the coffee table, sees the remote. For a minute she looks about to reach out, but the distance is perilously huge and she daren't.

Her palm is curled around a single fag: she puts it to her lips and moves her fingers until they're level with the pocket of her cardigan, eases out a box of matches. It is lit without mishap. She smokes with her hand at her face, not moving the cigarette, hearing the sigh and fizz of the tobacco as the end glows red hot with every drag. Someone comes into the room; Madeleine hears the sound of their heels, but she daren't look round. They leave without speaking.

Madeleine's cigarette tumbles ash down her front, and

the final draw on it tastes of the filter. For a moment, she's panicked, holding the filthy smoke-leaking thing away from her, and she leans forward all in a rush, and crushes it out in the ashtray, reckless. Then, she stands up with her heels against the front of her chair, so the ash drops to the floor without her having to touch it.

Now she's vulnerable to outside forces, standing all by herself in the smoke room. Madeleine lowers her body into the chair, rocking herself gently like a baby. It is at this moment that the television gets her. She can hear the pulsing of electricity through its umbilical cable, and the alien whiz of its brain. There's a flat, high keening coming from it, loud enough to tear things, audible only to Madeleine and to bats.

Madeleine knows she's lost now. For ten minutes at least, she resists, flicking her eyes around its heartless casing, concentrating on knobs or the reflections of adverts on the varnished coffee table. Eventually it's all too much, and she's pinned there, nailed by the eyes to the shifting faces and chaos of the screen. The ringing in her ears is amplified by the muzzy noise of static and the light bulb. She tries to think of something, something else, but there isn't anything; she's just a poor disconnected ear with nothing in its middle.

Then all at once someone flushes the loo outside, and people go past talking about food, and two big women with untidy hair invade Madeleine's dissolving nest. One of them, cruel as a goddess, strides past and snatches the remote control from the table as if it were nothing at all. They throw their backsides into chairs and turn the sound up high, and Madeleine begins, very quietly, to whimper.

MENDING

THE OTHER DAY, I went to a jumble sale at the ambulance station. You could buy jam jars full of marbles, and balls of knotty wool, and patent-leather handbags, and shoes that were worn down on one side of their soles. It was three o'clock; they were starting to stack the folding tables in the corner. The last one still up held all the useless things that were left and impossible to sell: unpairs of gloves and busted alarm clocks; pointless things, things only half-alive. They were so sad. I handed over three pound coins and took away a raggled heap of broken things in a shopping trolley.

At the top of the hill, I was out of puff, but the trolley stopped fighting me, and it was downhill from there to my house. The Tesco cart wouldn't go through the front door, so I opened the sash and shoved the broken things in armfuls through the window. Then I went in and stood in the living room gazing at my haul.

It was overwhelming; everything was so broken, and so many, that I couldn't bear to look at it all at once. I fled and sat at my kitchen table, gulping tea, while the broken things stayed silent in the living room, breathing evenly. I have made a mistake, I thought to myself; I have bitten off more than I can chew. There was so much to rescue in that drift of stuff; so many crippled things. When it got dark, I edged past the living room door and crept up the stairs. Then I sipped the dusty water in the glass beside my bed and slept; in my dreams there was the quiet sound of waiting.

I got up before the sun rose, and went to the broken things. I filled a mixing bowl with fragments and took them away to the kitchen table. With tweezers and superglue, I made myself a little mouse, with felty paws and a flickety wiry tail. She quivered in my hand whilst I threaded her fishing-line whiskers; I set her down on the mantelpiece to watch me.

After the mouse, I made three dozen others, out of bobs and bits of broken things, until the kitchen was alive with their tiny singing. The sun rose and fell again, and I went to bed.

The following day was shrill with the voices of mice; they had been at the pile of broken things during the night, and made themselves a whole tribe out of silver plate jewellery and shoelaces and spoons. When I looked in at the living room door, the heap was reduced by half. They sang all day and most of the night; the man who lived next door took to thumping on the walls. Their music was perfect and pointed as needles, like the nickel comb in a musical box. When I held out my arms, they came to me, and sat by the dozens in my lap. I whispered my life to the mice, and they listened.

By Wednesday there were mice and mice and mice; we spent weeks in the living room among the broken things, and we made a city from lampshades and a mildewy raincoat. The mice fashioned chairs and beds and baby mice, and the mantelpiece became a pedestrian thoroughfare. On the nesting tables we made a shopping mall, and they hollowed out the shelf of encyclopaedias for a hospital. The man next door shouted at me sometimes, through the walls.

The doorbell rang once at 4 a.m., and all the mice froze stiff with fright. The man next door was jealous; he held his face and snarled at us through the window, so we stapled old school uniforms over the glass. The mice made skirts and waistcoats from a flower-print bedspread, and paraded along the picture rail whilst their friends all clapped.

In the meantime, I became more mouse-like myself: every day I weighed a little less. I was pleased; soon I would be light as a cobweb. Whilst I awaited my transformation, I learned the dogwhistle language of mice.

It was not long until the pile of broken things was no longer there. Everything had now been used. The mice crowded around me with their questions: what was there now to rescue; with what should they make their young? For a moment, I was silent, cold with panic, but then the answer came to me like the voice of a rodent god.

When I started to break things for the mice, they all jumped in the air and cheered. I began in the kitchen; I held the knife handles over the end of the table and whacked them with the steam iron until I divided blade from wood. When I smashed up the radio there were a million bits inside, and the plates and cups crazed and snapped like bones.

I broke the taps off the sink and made a lake for the mice, a reservoir; within hours they were paddling little canoes up and down the linoleum floor, and by bedtime there was a steamboat. Someone knocked and knocked on the door for ages, but we pretended there was nobody in.

They came around the side of the house and looked in the kitchen window but we all stayed very still, until we were quite invisible.

I broke everything there was for the mice and finally ripped up the clothes on my back with my hands because the scissors were the archway entrance to the museum. My fur was growing by now, I was almost sure; the mirrors were in pieces, in use as solar panels, but the mice assured me that all was well. We were all so small and so light; I was as happy as any mouse could be. Everything was mending, becoming perfect and alive, with felty paws and flickety tails.

When they knocked the door down, when they made me come out, they ruined my world with their great nasty feet; trod my mice into sad raggled heaps of broken things.

ACKNOWLEDGEMENTS

THANKS ARE DUE to my agent, Victoria Hobbs; to the Arts Council England for Escalator funding and to George Szirtes for his endless time and encouragement. Thank you to Tobias Hill for the big break; to Kate Pullinger for mentoring; to Helen Ivory for the pizzas and ice-cream. Thank you to Andrea Porter; Caféwriters; Hilary Mellon; Caroline Forbes; Simon Miles; Barry Newman; the Bridges Creative Writing Group and Rethink; my sister Naomi and to Dawn Echlin, because she knows it's true. And thanks to my darling little girl, Jay.

Lightning Source UK Ltd.
Milton Keynes UK
UKOW04f0609081215

264269UK00002B/117/P